The Road That Winds Back

The Road That Winds Back

Elizabeth Hunt

Believer's Dream Publishing

All Rights Reserved. Published in the United States by Starlight Galaxy Publishing.

www.starlightgalaxypublishing.com

www.elizabethahunt.com

The text of this book is set in 12-point Avenir.
Printed in the United States of America

ISBN: 978-0-9832273-4-2

First edition

First printing, 2016

*For my teachers who taught me
these lessons*

Is fate unchangeable like a letter sent?

Does fate alone control life's path?

Can you meet fate and reach beyond,

to answer destiny's call?

For true power is found within

when fate is forgone to embrace the truth

of destiny's winding life path

The Road That Winds Back

α

Chapter 1

Five years ago, in the unlit winding backstreets of the city where I grew up, I was scurrying home from a late night grocery run.

Stopping for a moment, I struggled to catch my breath in the oppressively humid air. Between the humidity and sweat, my clothes were clinging to me in an uncomfortable manner and my dark hair was plastered to my head and neck. My muscles ached from the weight of the groceries.

I reached the corner before my house and sighed in relief. The one lone streetlight lit the driveway in an eerie orange glow as I walked towards the large iron gate that separates our house from the rest of the neighborhood.

In my arms the groceries were growing heavier, the burden seeming to grow with every step towards relieving myself of it. It was within the shadows cast by the wrought iron gate that I first heard the voice that would twist my life. The voice that appeared out of nowhere like it was born of the mist.

It said, "Alexandria."

I practically jumped out of my skin; to this day I don't know how I managed to keep hold of the groceries.

"Who's there?" I asked, hugging the groceries tighter to my body and backing up until my back was pressed against the gate.

The owner of the voice stepped into the light and I caught my breath.

It was a boy of about 17 with deeply tanned skin, straight black hair, and large brown eyes.

"Zahi?" I asked, incredulous.

Zahi had ridden at the same horse stable as me before his parents had passed on and he'd gone into the foster care system. We'd seen each other at least three times a week, and shown horses together on the weekends before then, but I hadn't heard from him since. The last time I had, he'd been so slight the wind could've blown him away. He was still slight, but there was something more substantial about his presence, like he was rooted to the earth. Far too solid to be a ghost at any rate.

"Alexandria, do you want to help spread peace in the world?" he asked.

I blinked several times, trying to make sense of what was going on. "Um... yes?" I replied.

Zahi nodded as if he'd been expecting me to say that. Though really I'd be surprised if anyone said anything else.

"You are going to be offered a scholarship soon for a boarding school far away. This school does not exist but accepting the offer will allow you to travel far and wide, spreading peace as far as you can. Pack nothing that you cannot carry easily."

Then as quickly as he had appeared, Zahi vanished into the shadows.

Breathing heavily, I looked around, wondering where he had gone. No one can truly vanish. Not really. Right?

Uneasily I unlocked the gate, not taking the time to admire the twisted metal flowers entwining into the bars or the metal animals welded to the bottom. The darkness seemed to close in on me as I ran the rest of the way up the driveway. There was a burning, ferocious, almost feral need flaring inside me to put as much distance between myself and the strange boy as possible. It was only when I'd gotten inside my house and locked the door tightly behind me that I remembered to breathe.

"Is that you, sweetie?"

"Yeah, mom, it's me," I wheezed, trying to adjust to the sudden normalcy of the situation.

"Oh good, bring the groceries to the kitchen. Your siblings are going to start a riot if they don't get fed soon."

I rolled my eyes and smiled. Standing straight, I shook my head slightly as if to dislodge the creepy encounter and set off towards the kitchen.

The house was not large per se, but it was well-sized with three stories and 11 rooms. I walked past the staircase and kept going to the back of the house where my mother stood facing the window and washing her hands in the sink. From the doorway I could see my reflection next to my mother's as if we were standing side by side. The similarities were endless, but my eyes are a mix of green and blue that make them appear almost gray, like the sea on a cold winter day, while my mother's eyes are brown as the chocolate she pretends not to eat.

"Right here on the table," my mother said, gesturing towards the spot with her slightly soapy hand.

I strode forward and set the bags down gently on top of the pale wood tabletop. It was a relief to be rid of the weight and I shook my arms several times to convince the blood to flow back into my fingertips.

"Thanks, sweetie, I think I can handle dinner so why don't you head up and finish your homework or whatever it is you need to do."

I nodded and turned around, heading back out into the long hall to the staircase. The dark wood floors seemed almost black with the lights off, the white moulding on the beige walls acting like runway lights to guide me on my way.

Up the staircase, hang a right, down the hall a bit and into my room. I could find my way there blindfolded. I had lived in this house my whole life and I knew every nook and cranny.

With a sigh I collapsed on my twin bed, spreading my hands out to feel the comforting texture of the duvet cover. My homework had been done for hours now—I had finished it before I'd even left school. Below I heard several doors slam as my brother and sister raced about the house doing who knows what.

Lying there, what I was trying not to do was think of Zahi.

It was an illusion. It was dark and my overly sensitive imagination was working overtime. Nothing is going to happen. You're fine.

By the time my mother called me for dinner, I had almost convinced myself.

{[|][|][|][|]}

Dinner was always a rather noisy affair. My father regaled us with tales of his day at work while my siblings interjected with stories of their own, sometimes simultaneously. That night we had mashed potatoes, chicken and peas, so it wasn't long before the twins were making sculptures.

"How was your day, Alexandria?" my father asked, eyeing Isaac's mashed potato monster with raised eyebrows.

"The same," I replied. I didn't mention Zahi, I didn't mention the letter from a mythical school I was supposed to receive. I didn't mention any of it. Parents tend to freak out about stuff like that.

"That's nice dear. Nicolas, attend to your son!" My mother reprimanded my father who had allowed Isaac to fling peas at Rachel. While my mother consoled my sister and my father scolded her twin brother, I got up and took my plate to the dish washer. I was more than ready to escape to my bedroom away from the antics of the ten-year olds.

"Oh, Alexandria, there's mail for you on the front table dear."

"'Kay!"

I walked down the hall and grabbed the mail before taking the stairs two at a time and disappearing into my bedroom.

Sitting down at my desk I began flipping through the magazines carelessly and sorting through the college brochures that had been arriving with increasing frequency, though it was still early for me to be applying anywhere. It was the last envelope that made me pause.

It was plain manila, but the return address was a school I had never heard of, not uncommon, but I didn't recognize the location either.

Chapter 1

I opened the letter with trembling hands and read what it had to say.

Miss Alexandria Maria Del Mare,

We have written to inform you that you have been accepted at Dacia's Academy for the Sighted. We urge you to accept this once in a lifetime opportunity to broaden your mind and learn how you can change the world and the Universe. Term starts September 5th when you leave on the 3 o'clock train from your nearest station.

With all regards,

Dacia

Director of Admissions

I put down the letter with trembling hands. This mystery school did not exist. I was sure of it. For one thing, no one would make a special school for the "sighted". They made special schools for the blind. For another, this Dacia person who claimed to be the director of admissions a) had no last name and b) was obviously also the founder of this so called school since it was named after her.

It was just too suspicious to be real. But if the school wasn't real...that meant seeing Zahi *was* real.

I put my head in my hands and tried to make sense of it all. It had been a long day and my wits were frayed. What in the world could this possibly mean? What was real? What was going on?

{[|][|][|][|]}

Over the next several days I did my best to push the events of that night out of my mind. If I didn't think about it, it couldn't happen. Right? The problem was I couldn't stop thinking about it. At all. Every minute of every day the illusion of Zahi appearing in the night haunted me. At night I found myself pulling the school letter out of the trash and staring it, willing it to provide me with the answers I so desperately craved.

Just when I had managed to convince myself I had dreamed of Zahi and the letter was simply a coincidence, *she* showed up. Dacia. The woman whose "school" I was invited to join. I came home from high school that day to find her in the living room talking to my parents. Upon sight I knew who she was. Don't ask me how, because I don't know. But she was there. And she was there for me.

"Alexandria, I'm glad you're home," my father began. "Dacia here was just telling us about a scholarship you won. Why didn't you tell us you wanted to go to an elite boarding school for the gifted?"

Underneath the question I could hear an accusation. What my father really wanted to ask was "Why do you want to leave?".

I longed to tell my father the truth. That I had applied for no scholarship and the school wasn't real. At least, not according to my mysterious ghost boy. But as I stood there in the hall, my backpack still slung over my shoulder, I couldn't find the words.

Dacia saved me. "It was not a scholarship for which one applies," she said. "My school is highly selective and seeks out its applicants on its own." She looked right at me and in that instant I knew that somehow or another, whether I wanted to or not, I would end up at her mysterious "school." That was my path.

I don't think I have ever been as scared as I was that night. Even in all my adventures since, I have never felt as paralyzed and unsure as when I stood on the brink of the unknown there in my hallway with my parents and a complete stranger. For the first time I took a good look at Dacia. She had wild white hair, largely uncontained by her short ponytail, larger than life blue eyes, and a gaze that pierced right through you. I had a feeling she knew exactly what I was thinking and feeling—that I wasn't sure about this.

"Alexandria is a very special and gifted girl," Dacia said as she left. "I hope she considers this unique opportunity." Then she turned and said very seriously, "It's only offered once in a lifetime, Alexandria. I know it's hard to start a new path, but sometimes it's necessary." I knew she meant it.

{[|][|][|][|]}

Sometimes I feel the need to write, to get my thoughts down before they can escape, to create some record of what's whizzing through my head at the speed of light and try to make sense of it all. That night was one of those moments. For hours, I sat at my desk, at my computer, typing, writing with ink and paper, spewing my thoughts onto pages and pages.

Chapter 1

My thoughts and feelings had never before been so vastly out of control as they were at that moment. I knew, without a shadow of a doubt, that my parents would send me to Dacia's mysterious school. The school that didn't exist. All her talk of me being special, gifted, of being the next super-genius. They had believed every word, hung on to every sentence. Even though my parents loved me and hated to spend any amount of time apart from me, Dacia had convinced them so thoroughly of my brilliance as to make them think that I could never be happy anywhere else but at her made up school. Where I could "socialize" with other youth of my "excellent calibre."

The thoughts I spewed all tried to answer the basic question: why. Why was Dacia so determined that I go with her? Was she a pedophile? A kidnapper? Some doctor who needed teenagers for inhumane experiments? I wanted to believe all of those things. If those things were true, I could find the police, I could find help, I could get out of leaving the comforts of home.

But in my heart, I knew that there was no getting out of this. Not now. Not ever. My road lay before me, clear as daylight and the truth was I was too scared to take that path. The unknown is like an abyss, spiraling away and upward towards an uncertain end. No so-called normal person who values their life would jump into that abyss. Would they?

In this fashion I stayed up all night, writing, deleting, re-writing, reaching the same conclusions again and again like a computer doing a math equation.

I remembered Zahi's words, "Pack nothing you can't carry easily." and I remembered the words Dacia had whispered to me as she left, "Never forget, you *are* gifted and special, Alexandria. We have chosen you to serve the Universe for a reason and I promise you will not regret any of your travels with us."

They made it sound as if I was suddenly the heroine of a novel, or a television drama, or a movie, or something. But I wasn't any of those things. I was just a girl. An ordinary girl with an ordinary life. Two parents, two siblings, a roof over my head, food to eat, a good education, friends... I was a very privileged girl. Heroines in stories, they are never well off. They're orphaned, or their parents are divorced, or they are bullied, made fun of, down on their luck...*something* has happened to them where they are misfortunate. I was quite the opposite. And perhaps that's why I found it so hard to believe.

"Honey?" My mother interrupted my thoughts sometime later. I was lying on my bed, staring at the ceiling, thinking the same thoughts over and over again when she sat down on the blankets. "I know this is all a bit sudden, sweetheart, but this elite boarding school really sounds like a great opportunity for you."

"What about my life here, Mom? My friends, my family, my horse..."

"You'll see us on holiday and you'll make new friends," my mother reassured me. "As for your horse I'm sure we can work something out. Dacia did mention having a very extensive equestrian program."

I just lay back on my bed and covered my head. The school didn't exist. This was all part of the illusion. It couldn't possibly have an equestrian program.

"It'll be fun, sweetie. Just you wait."

{[]][]][]][]]}

In the end, I was to take my horse with me. The only reason I could figure was maybe

Dacia was a nomad and I would need some way to get around with her. It had been nearly two months since Dacia had come to my doorstep and convinced my parents to let me go with her. Now there I stood, surrounded by people but completely alone, on a train platform with my luggage by my feet and my parents off by the ticket stand making the finishing touches for my journey.

My horse, Ace, was loaded into the train's livestock car, and my luggage was stowed. In a few short moments I would board the train and my life would find a new purpose. My path was disappearing into the fog and Dacia and Zahi would teach me how to find it again. I hoped.

As instructed I was leaving at 3 o'clock from the train station closest to my house, which according to the map would take me to a small town just outside of Sydney.

The train whistle blew loudly and a rush of bodies began pressing in on me, all trying to get on the train as fast as they could. I stood there, staring at the dark green car in front of me, willing myself anywhere else in the Universe. I was falling into the frightening abyss of the unknown even as I desperately scrambled for something to hold on to—anything to keep me from plummeting to the depths.

"Come on, let's get you on the train," my father murmured in my ear. My mother grabbed my hand and pulled me along, the two of them getting me on the train and situated in a compartment before kissing me on the head and leaving.

It was several more minutes before the train would pull out of the station, so I stared out the window, watching my parents as they waved enthusiastically, hiding any sadness or worry they might feel about sending me off on my own. Part of me wished they didn't, I wanted to know just how much they would miss me.

With another loud whistle, the train began chugging away, faster and faster, leaving the platform behind. As I watched my parents faces disappear into the fog of the steam engine, I couldn't help but let a tear escape. I watched my reflection in the window as it trickled down my cheek and onto the book in my lap. I had a feeling I wouldn't be seeing my parents for an extraordinarily long time and that was a thought I did not want to face.

β

Chapter 2

It was nightfall when the train finally reached the small Australian village, nestled in a valley in the outback and nearly a hundred miles from any true civilization. Up in the sky, the stars shone bright and glorious—not a single cloud, natural or smog, to mar their shine. I took a deep breath of the clean, fresh, humid air and felt peaceful for the first time that day. The air clung to me like a blanket giving me a sense of security that was quickly abolished by the other passengers as they disembarked, shoving me about in the masses.

"Alexandria!"

I whipped around at the sound of my name coming from none other than my personal ghost. His slight frame maneuvered expertly through the crowd until he was standing right next to me. I noted with surprise that he was at least a head taller than me now—when we were little he'd always been at least a head shorter.

"You have your luggage?" Zahi asked, his voice raised to be heard above the din.

I nodded, the words getting stuck deep in my throat.

"Follow me. Dacia's at the livestock cars unloading your horse."

Zahi began moving back through the crowd again with my luggage, but I hesitated in following him. Even now, I could just get back on the train and keep going, away from this unknown mystery and go back home where I knew what life held. If I followed Zahi, that was it, I would plunge into the dark abyss of the unknowns. *I've made it this far,* I thought, then I mustered my courage and followed him.

{[l][l][l][l]}

The next morning was our first day of "school." We woke up at dawn and ate a quick breakfast of something mushy and then got to work building houses until the heat of the afternoon and the blazing sun demanded we seek shelter. For the remainder of the afternoon we meditated in our tiny hut, practically steaming as the sweat rolled down our backs. As I meditated I decided that I wasn't so much in a school as I was on a mission trip type activity. However, after I came to this realization, the meditation became quite boring. Surely there was something more productive we could be doing instead of sitting around in a daze. I didn't understand the benefits of meditation yet and my perceptions were so wrong it's laughable.

"Relax, Alexandria. Release your thoughts and find peace. Let them flow through your consciousness," Dacia said, raising an eyebrow at my fidgeting. It just wasn't that easy. I could meditate for maybe for ten minutes at first, then an hour as I got used to it. But we meditated from when we stopped working until dinnertime and sometimes that encompassed some six hours.

I could not understand the point or stay relaxed that long. Everything I had ever been taught previously encouraged me to do something productive every minute of every day. I didn't understand at the time that meditation is productive. Just not in the usual societal ways. As the days grew hotter and we retired to shade earlier and earlier, we began doing yoga, specifically sun salutation, interspersed with our meditation.

By the twentieth day of this schedule, I finally began to appreciate the stillness, peace and tranquility of soul, mind, and body the mindfulness of meditation brought, and the connection yoga forms between body and mind. Dacia had been right, though I hadn't been listening at the time. The point of meditation was to release your thoughts into the collective consciousness of the world and recuperate.

On the thirtieth day, we finished the first home. I missed my parents. But it had been a month and I'd grown used to my new life. I had friends helping to build the houses who actually were on a mission trip.

I wasn't particularly happy we'd finished because that meant the mission group was leaving. I wasn't sure how I felt about being alone with Dacia and Zahi, but I had realized that there is something incredibly energizing about both the physical exercise of building and the emotional reward of seeing the families appreciate the work.

The smiling faces of the villagers when they looked upon their new home gave me a sense of grounding myself to the earth and finding peace with the world. So despite my qualms, I knew I wouldn't leave with everyone else but would stay and finish what I started.

The first afternoon we were alone I discovered meditation can be a way to reconnect to the heart and the heartbeat of the earth around us and a path to fully appreciate our place in the universe.

It was a mental breakthrough. After that, I began to understand how to find peace and how to meditate in any situation. I learned to feel the penetrating sun on my back, the cool breeze on my skin as it raised goosebumps, and in my gut I began to sense the vibration of the world around me. Day by day Zahi and I learned and we adapted.

Being on our own at the construction site wasn't too bad. We all moved into the meditation cabin and the family into their house and we began building another one for the next family over.

And now mixed into the meditation and the yoga were the lessons. The lessons Dacia taught us planted seeds in our minds and it was our responsibility to water them and help them grow. The first lesson taught us how we should live in the present moment and avoid dwelling on the past or future. The meditation was a key part of that.

The second lesson taught us how we should appreciate the people around us. That came in handy when the second mission group came down to help us. They were obnoxious. But we learned to overlook their personalities and appreciate their intent.

And in our third lesson, the purpose of the "mystery school" finally became clear in my mind. It wasn't too long after we finished our third house. We were alone again—winter was approaching and the mission groups had slowly stopped coming.

"Alexandria," Dacia called. Her voice was never stern, never raised above a normal tone, but somehow she could always be heard, even in the stables. Even with the screeching falcons wheeling overhead and the hoof beats of horses surrounding me, Dacia could say my name all the way across the arena and still be heard.

I stopped looking out over the desert and crossed the room to sit cross legged in front of Dacia on a hard, square cushion, accepting the cup of steaming herbal tea she offered me.

"What do you know of the energetic chakra system of the body?"

"Chakras?" I asked surprised. "I don't know. Is it part of your aura?" I'd heard those terms in reference to each other before.

Dacia bowed her head. "The chakras find roots in many cultures, many religions, and many spheres of this universe. It originated as a Buddhist idea and expanded into Hinduism and beyond. It was a Buddhist man who first described their hierarchy.

"The heart chakra is centric to the system. If your heart chakra is blocked you have a hardened heart and a hardened heart does not feel. Learning about the chakras will help you release the blocks that prevent your energy from flowing. I brought you here, Alexandria, to make a difference in the world, but to truly do that you have to understand the heart and how the heart serves people.

Suddenly I understood what she was getting at. The peace I felt at the end of the day, the tranquility and security I felt was because my heart chakra was in balance.

"What about the rest of the Chakras?"

Dacia shook her head. "You will know in time. That is why you are here, Alexandria. To train to be like us, to help and serve people. Zahi is learning to feel this too." I looked over at my old friend and wondered, for the first time, just how long he'd been wandering about with Dacia, learning. Somehow knowing he'd been at this awhile and was fine helped calm any anxiety I still had.

"So how long does it take?"

"What do you mean, Alexandria?"

"How long does it take to understand what we're learning? To truly help people grow?"

Dacia smiled. "You never stop learning Alexandria. But how long it takes you to understand the multidimensional, universal laws well enough to serve... Well that is entirely dependent on you, and how well you listen. One day you will be able to see. And then you'll wake up."

I mulled that information over for days becoming so caught up in it that I began to stop noticing the physical world around me. I didn't notice the birds wheeling through the sky or the clouds as they drifted this way and that.

I was becoming blocked in my mind, in a constant state of an unhealthy split-minded meditation as I concentrated and pondered. I began riding Ace further and further away each day, seeking something I could not name; the sadness growing in my heart every day it did not appear.

{[|][|][|][|]}

At this point, it had been nearly six months since I'd last seen my parents. I had talked to them on the phone—the few times I got signal—and letters were regularly exchanged, but I was beginning to miss them terribly. It was like a hollow ache in my chest when I thought about them, living a so-called "normal" suburbia life. It was hard for me to realize that they weren't learning like I was. That they hadn't woken up, that they were still stuck in their place, oblivious to the many dimensions that encircled our own and it was hard for me that they weren't by my side as they had been my entire life. It was like I'd gone to college early and I'm not sure I was entirely ready for that.

Sometimes the urge to leave rose up like bile. I wanted to flee; go back home and find them, tell them everything I was learning. But then I would feel the sun's dancing rays, hear the song of the wind, relax into the heartbeat of mother earth and start to embrace the wonders of nature. I would remember why I chose to stay.

In my mind and soul, I was starting to understand what Dacia meant when she said how long it took to learn the universal laws depended on my choices. To be open to understanding, I had to practice. It took patience to interpret the truths and knowledge of life.

My eyes would never see if I closed them, if I stayed in the ego. I couldn't judge. I couldn't crave. I could just experience and observe. And that's a very hard thing to do.

Whenever my ego tried to deny what was happening to me and my life, whenever that ego began to try and make things go my way, that's when I would start seeing the world upside down—like most of the people who inhabit it. Denial is so prevalent and it hinders the ability to connect to our hearts and see the world for the beauty that abounds.

Centering my thoughts became a skill. There was a certain amount of selfish thought my ego was allowed before I started feeling lost in this universe. When I don't think a single selfish, ego-centered thought, that's when I feel truly grounded. That's when the world suddenly starts to make sense for all its vastness. As I got better at centering myself, and embraced what I had instead of yearning for what I didn't, the hole in my heart began to fill in. I still missed my parents, but it was no longer crippling me.

There is a paradigm that sums this up quite nicely: as long as love, forgiveness, and grace abound, everything seems brighter.

Dacia and Zahi's enjoyment of the world was contagious. It wore off on me. They helped embody the paradigm.

Zahi and I quickly fell into friendship like we'd had years ago and when we had a day off, we went riding together to explore the surrounding outback and discover new paths. There was something amazing and uplifting about uncovering the beauty of the wild. Just to see the beauty of it all brought me a sense of belonging that cities never can.

It was on one of these outings that I first saved a life. It wasn't planned—these things never are—but it came naturally. And that's what I was learning in my lessons. The best way to be a hero. For that's what we were trying to be: hidden heroes.

{[][][][]}

On the day in question, Zahi and I were out riding along the deep, rushing river, further out then we'd ever been before. We had just considered stopping to water the horses and grab some lunch when the wind changed, bringing with it a sharp, malodorous scent.

"What is that?" I reined in Ace and turned my nose into the breeze, trying to identify the harrowing stench that was making my stomach turn in knots and my heart race.

"Smoke," Zahi answered, suddenly tense.

Together we began scanning the horizon, looking for the source of the smoke. We intuitively recognized the smoky smell as no ordinary bonfire. There was something unsettling about it that set our nerves on edge.

"There!" I shouted after a minute, pointing towards the copse of trees in the distance where plumes of smoke were beginning to appear. As Zahi and I watched the smoke on the horizon, it began to intensify, thickening and turning blacker.

"That's a large fire," I whispered as we watched the smoke grow higher.

The sight was so captivating, I'm not sure we would've remembered to move if we hadn't heard the scream. As it penetrated through the air we were brought back to reality and we galloped towards the fire.

When we drew close, the stench of the smoke was thick and choking so we dismounted and began to crawl near the ground where the smoke was thinner until we found the source of the flames.

A house, two stories tall, that had been previously painted yellow and white was surrounded by the yellow orange embers of a raging fire. Most of the house was already aflame but one corner was still untouched. For now.

Zahi and I reached the side of the house downwind of the smoke and stood up, running over to the gathering of people.

"What happened?" I asked as soon as we were in ear shot.

At the question one of the older women with graying hair and a faded apron began to sob while a younger girl that appeared to be her daughter comforted her. It was the man that finally spoke, "I think the fire began in the kitchen based on the way the flames are spreading. My wife and I were out gathering wood when our daughter came running through the woods to tell us the house was alight. She herself was in her bedroom when she smelled the smoke."

"Is there anyone still in there?" Zahi asked urgently as a loud cracking noise from the house announced structural failure.

"We don't know."

"How can you not know?" I asked eyeing the house with fright, already imagining the burnt corpses.

"We were all out doing chores. I don't know who had come back already," the man explained.

"Well wouldn't your daughter know?" Zahi pressed gesturing to the girl.

The man shook his head. "She's deaf. She wouldn't have heard them come back."

It was too much for me, I began running around the house, shouting if anyone was inside, scanning all the windows for any sign of life. When I reached the back of the house where the smoke was thickest but the house relatively untouched, Zahi caught up to me.

"Alexandria, what are you doing?" he asked with a cough.

"We have to find out if anyone's in there!" I yelled back. "We can't leave them trapped."

"Don't you think they would have gotten our attention by now if they were?" Zahi responded logically.

But I was beyond reason, my eyes continued scanning every inch of the house, absorbing everything I could as fast as I could.

"There," I finally said. "The curtain fluttered. There's someone in there."

"It's probably just the smoke Alexandria," Zahi wheezed. The smoke was too thick to see through at this point and I had to cough several times before I could speak. "No, I'm certain I saw something."

And before Zahi could stop me, I ran up to the tree by the house and began climbing as fast as I could, breathing through my shirt but still inhaling too much smoke. I knew I was being reckless but I also knew I'd seen *something* in the window. I couldn't stand to wait helplessly below and then find the corpses.

By the time I broke the glass and tumbled through the window, the fire had reached the far corner of the room. I could feel the heat searing through the door and prayed that whatever I had seen was indeed in this room because there was no way to get to any of the others.

"Hello?" I called before collapsing in a violent coughing fit; the smoke was nearly impossible to breathe now.

A small whimper met my inquiry and I whipped around. Right beside the window was a young boy, no more than ten, curled into a ball, pale and shaky, struggling to breathe just as I was.

"Hold on," I cried as I knelt beside him. "I'm here to help you out. We're going to get you out." I kept talking as I got him onto his feet. I climbed onto the windowsill and out onto the nearest branch, helping the boy out behind me. He was weak and couldn't stop coughing from prolonged exposure to the smoke, but he could move.

"Come on, come on," I urged as I watched the fire creeping across the floor of the room towards us. I heard voices below me crying out from the ground and knew the family had come around the house. We were almost to the trunk of the tree when a loud crack sounded and the roof of the house collapsed, spraying hot embers towards the boy and myself.

The boy stifled a sob of fear and I felt my heart clench. I looked up into the sky and prayed that he had been the only one left in the house.

We reached the ground and the sobbing woman enveloped the two of us in a hug, clinging to the small boy and mumbling in another language repeatedly as she looked him over.

"Thank you, thank you," she said to me in English after she was sure her son was going to be all right. Another crack sounded from within the house and the three of us hurried away towards the now significantly larger group. Several burly men had shown up and were lugging water from the well and showering it onto the flames repeatedly while the family was joined by three more children all looking fearful but safe. The boy was quickly enveloped by the rest of his family.

"Thank you again and again for rescuing our son," the man said through tears. "We had no way of knowing who was in there but now we know everyone is safe. Thank you, thank you."

"It's no problem," I muttered sheepishly, looking at my feet. It felt weird to be praised so since I hadn't done it for the attention. But I knew as I looked at the reunited family that there was not a power on this earth that would be able to stop me from helping the world. Not now and not ever.

γ

Chapter 3

When we told Dacia what happened, she nodded at my bold rescue of the child.

"Were you scared, Alexandria?" she asked.

I nodded.

"What were you scared of?"

I thought that over for a minute. "I was scared someone would get hurt, or burn in the fire and be lost."

"But you weren't scared for yourself?"

I shook my head. It sounds reckless to not be scared for my own life. But it was true. I hadn't really stopped to consider the dangers. "I knew that it was the right thing to do, if there was someone trapped by the fire...letting them die was just not an option."

Dacia seemed to understand. She looked at me carefully and then said in a measured voice. "Alexandria, you have now not only shown compassion for those around you, but you have truly saved a life, and so I am going to ask you a question."

I nodded and waited for Dacia to continue.

"Zahi and I are going to move on soon. Our mission in this town is nearing its conclusion. You have begun your lessons and if you choose, you can go back home instead of traveling with us. You can go back to your old high school and live a suburban life, or you can travel with us and keep learning about the laws of the universe. If you do, someday you will be able to truly help and serve people with compassion as you did today."

I thought about the hollow ache in my heart and about my family. I missed them terribly, but they were safe, and they loved me. I knew someday I would go home, but there are too many other families that aren't safe and that need help. I had made a vow to myself, if could help, then I would.

"I want to travel with you," I answered Dacia.

"Well then you better start packing," she said with a wink.

{[][][][][]}

The next morning, our belongings were neatly stowed away in bags and slung over the backs of a couple horses. When Dacia told me we would always travel by horse, I gave her a funny look. No one had traveled by horse in decades, I told her. It was old fashioned. But Dacia just gave me her "you'll see" look and walked off to inspect the packing efforts.

Leaving was a slow, quiet affair; around midday we finally mounted up and set off, no fanfares, no goodbyes; just gone like the wind. No one would say where we were going, I'm not sure they even knew. We were becoming highly nomadic, wandering from place to place. Dacia said we were searching for learning opportunities. I think she was looking for adventure.

After a couple weeks, however, I began to question where we were headed. I was tired of wandering. Plus, by my calculations we should have arrived at a city by now, or the ocean. But there were no cities in sight for miles on end and any water was devoid of salt. It was unnatural, we were headed east, we should've found *something*. When I brought this up to Zahi one afternoon he just rolled his eyes.

"We're traveling, Alexandria," he replied. That's the only answer I ever got. Whenever I questioned the terrain or the sky or anything that seemed unnatural to me I always got the same answer. "We're traveling." As if that made perfect sense.

As the days passed I felt myself becoming lost again—as if the ground was slowly lifting away from beneath my feet letting me float along, unhinged and unprotected. It was an eerie, otherworldly effect and I could feel fear creeping in on me at all times. The fear that we were lost, doomed to roam the countryside forevermore, the fear that no one knew what they were doing, the fear that I had made the wrong decision in agreeing to come along.

When we finally reached a village, it wasn't one I recognized. The black smog was chokingly thick, the buildings grimy and graffitied, dominating and monolithic. The people were scarce and starved. Their hair was patchy and dirty, their clothes naught but rags, and their skin black with soot from the air and the fires that burned in the trash bins.

"Where are we," I whispered, appalled as we passed a family living in a box who looked more skeleton then human. I'd read about places on the earth where people lived in poverty and desolate conditions but I had never imagined such a horror as this place. It was like the apocalypse had come and gone leaving naught but the last dregs of humanity behind.

Dacia reined her horse, Paco, in so that she was walking next to me and said simply, "We have passed into a lower realm. We're in the factory district. These few people are unfit to work. Everyone else spends twelve hours or more a day operating the machinery in these buildings."

I gazed with alarm at the monoliths and imagined the people within, sweaty and dark with machinery oil and grease, working without cease to create whatever luxuries might be produced. Then Dacia's words really sank in.

"What do you mean, "a lower realm"?" I asked, suspiciously.

Dacia was silent for a long while, but at last she spoke. "Have you ever heard of Yggdrasil?"

I racked my memory for any mention of the word. "The tree in Norse Mythology?"

Dacia smiled. "Very good. Do you remember anything about it?"

"It was like a map," I said, struggling to remember. "Climbing up and down the tree you could reach any domain in Norse mythology, from Valhalla to Niflheim."

Dacia nodded. "Close enough. And do you remember where humans lived?"

"In Middle earth, on the ground near the base of the tree before you descended into the roots and below the branches."

"We're traveling similar paths," Dacia stated. "Conceptually almost the same paths," she muttered as an afterthought.

I struggled to comprehend what she meant. "So, we're traveling to different worlds?"

"If that's how you wish to think of it. They are more often referred to as different dimensions, however." Dacia replied. "We have come to this place to find your missing soul piece and heal you."

I looked to the side of the desolate street at the graffiti screaming "help" whose once bright red lettering had nearly faded into obscurity. How could such a place heal me?

Dacia seemed to sense my confusion. "Zahi," she called. "Tell Alexandria where we are."

Dacia rode forward and let Zahi drop back.

"We are where pain and suffering endure," Zahi whispered to me.

"I think I got that part," I muttered back as a gaunt man came into sight. He was talking to the bricks like they were old friends.

Zahi shook his head. "Alexandria, everyone is wounded. Sometimes the wounds go back millennia, other times they are from childhood. One of my wounds was my parent's death."

"Nothing traumatic has ever happened to me," I argued. But I knew that wasn't true, trauma has many forms.

Zahi shook his head again. "Alexandria we will help you," he said. "A wound, it can be healed. But first it must be found. We are here to find your wound, your pain and suffering. In time you will find it, and then with time it will heal."

"How do you even know I'm wounded?" I snapped grumpily.

"Everyone is wounded, Alexandria, I told you. It affects how you see the world, it affects how you see yourself. It affects what you project to others. A person's wound shapes all the negative aspects of their personality, like shame and guilt."

"Where *are* we, Zahi?" I insisted, ignoring what he said.

Zahi pursed his lips, but he answered. "We are in one of the lower worlds. It represents the past and the lower energy root chakras. Various mythologies often depict it as a site of evil and darkness."

The familiar fear was pervading my every sense by this point and I couldn't think straight to save my life, so I nudged Ace and rode ahead until I was halfway between Zahi and Dacia and sandwiched between the pack horses, alone with my thoughts and the dull sound of hoofbeats on the road.

Everything that had just come out of Zahi and Dacia's mouths was complete nonsense. Dimension traveling, generational or childhood wounds, none of it could be true. But at the same time everything they said made perfect sense.

We were in the exactly the right place to find my wound. The trauma of the encounter that haunted my darkest nightmares was fresh in my mind and yet, I refused to believe a word of what Zahi said because I was just plain scared. I had no wish to relive the traumatic experience and had a feeling that that was exactly what was going to happen.

So I stewed, and blamed everyone but myself. I was angry, fearful, resentful and stubborn. Now, I can admit that every single word out of Zahi's mouth that day was true. But at the time I would have slapped anyone who even suggested listening more closely. I was in denial and disconnected from my heart.

That was how scared I was. Fear makes people do terrible things. That is an important lesson not to forget. When someone's behavior doesn't make sense, look at their fears. Denial and other irrational thoughts or behaviors tend to spring from fear.

Though I do maintain to this day that my fear on that day was perfectly rational because I was right: when I discovered my wound, it was because I relived it and that is perhaps one of the most terrifying things I've ever done in my life.

{[][][][][]}

As we walked our horses down the street, the visages of horror continued to assail our senses. It got to the point where I almost couldn't remember what peace or happiness were. To save myself from the sight of one particularly gruesome scene, I averted my gaze to the nearest building upon which someone had graffitied three distinct initials. A. dM.

My initials.

Alexandria del Mare.

Subconsciously I steered Ace right up to the letters, staring at them as if I could somehow glean their purpose from the chipped and peeling paint.

"I think we're supposed to go in," I murmured, frozen by the thought. This building was the most decrepit I had seen yet and looked disconcertingly familiar. If this building housed the trauma of my past I wanted to ride as fast as I could in the opposite direction.

Yet I found myself dismounting, running my hand along the initials as I made my way towards the door. Zahi and Dacia didn't utter a word of protest. They simply followed; Zahi a little tentative. In my mind, a battle was taking place; curiosity for what lay ahead fighting against my knowledge that it would be nothing good. It was like watching a horror movie, when you want to know what happens but are afraid to keep watching.

As I crept inside the building, my first thought was I should wash my hands. The filth and grime covered everything and stuck to you like crazy glue. The wooden stairs were rotting and drooped dangerously while what paint that once existed was powder on the edges of the room's entrance.

I made my way to the rotting stairs, following some internal compass that was coercing me forward. Before attempting to climb the stairs, however, I hesitated—surely they were too dangerous to use. But the desire to know what was upstairs was unquenchable, so I mustered my courage and kept to the wall side of the staircase where I thought the nails would be.

The only sound came from the muted sounds of my footsteps and the creaking of the wooden stairs. It was utterly eerie.

Zahi and Dacia remained by the door, though Zahi gave a restrained whimper of concern when the stairs let out a particularly frightening crack. When I reached the top of the stairs, however, the second story was in better shape than I'd imagined. The wood and paint and smell were the same but the grime was minimal and the dust practically nonexistent in what had clearly once been a maze of office cubicles.

Entranced, I ducked under the caution tape roping off the room and wove through various tattered, plastic drop cloths to examine the area. Most of the office cubicles were empty and all were in differing states of disrepair—some could be classified as merely shabby while others were clearly condemned. After passing a cubicle that played host to a family of vicious rats, I was pleasantly surprised to find a cubicle whose only negative characteristic was its evident age— the faded, peeling paint job, the rotting cork board, and the ratty fabric walls indicated the small square area of space hadn't been used for at least a decade.

Again, I was struck by a sense of familiarity and found myself wandering into the cubicle to open various drawers. The first one contained what might have been a mouse nest: lots of shredded paper and stuffing covered with a thin layer of droppings. The second drawer was empty apart from a spider or two and some cobwebs. But the third drawer had a picture. Faded with time and water marked, the image was blurry but clear enough for me to see the subject: a little girl and her father on a swing set. The little girl's face was obscured by a splotch, but her little hands were in her father's large ones and his face was one of such protective love, I was momentarily taken aback. This little girl had meant everything to her father.

Tears welled in my eyes as I remembered my own father. Why was this picture here, in this hell hole, all alone and abandoned? It made me wonder what had happened. What had gone wrong that this photo was left sitting in a drawer? What had made this precious moment either worth leaving or not worth remembering?

"Who's there?!" A deep voice reverberated around the room. My hands shook and my breath and heartbeat quickened alarmingly as my adrenaline spiked. Instinctively, I dropped the photo and ran, faster and faster, always aware of the footsteps closing in.

{[|][|][|][|]}

I remember only flashes and glimpses of the following sequence. It's like trying to remember a nightmare. Everything is disjointed and jumpy, the details blurring together until I remember appearing in different parts of the room without moving.

Memory is weird like that, deleting those details it finds unnecessary and leaving a jumbled mess of confusion. Very rarely does one remember an event being both good and bad. The memory usually denotes the scene as one or the other based on the ratio of high points to low points. More high points during the event leaves a good memory. An abundance of low points leaves a bad memory. Perhaps that's why our ideals are typically black and white. It's hard to remember things as grey.

At any rate, I do remember running. Running so fast and focused that I didn't notice where I was or where I was going. I remember hearing my breath coming out in pants and the footsteps and labored breathing of my pursuer, but I never looked back. I was afraid to see what was following me. I was afraid it would see my face and remember it.

I recall crouching in a cubicle and seeing the shadow of feet as I peered under the partition and through a plastic sheet. I remember crab crawling backwards as fast as I could, trying to find the exit while not being found.

I remember being extra careful not to make any noise and then bumping into a box with a rat nest sending them flying and causing a racket that sent my heart thumping even faster as I bolted again.

I remember the shot, the impact and the chipped wood as I flew past, tripping over my own feet and pitching face first down the stairs.

I remember Zahi catching me and yelling incoherently as I dragged him and Dacia back out onto the street.

I remember mounting Ace and riding away as fast as she would carry me.

It wasn't until we were past the town and into the polluted countryside that I reined Ace in, looking at everything as if it was preparing to attack.

"What have you learned, Alexandria?" Dacia asked softly after a while, studying me with her knowing, piercing gaze.

I shivered involuntarily. I wasn't ready to talk about what had happened. Even at the time, I recognized that I was probably overreacting—the man chasing me probably meant no harm. But I couldn't help my reaction. I couldn't tell my adrenaline to stop pumping.

"That was my wound," I murmured, not quite ready to talk about it.

Zahi looked at me strangely.

"What?" I snapped.

"You've always run from authority," he said, his eyes lost in thoughts of the past. "You never asked questions when you thought the answer would be no. You never took a risk if it could get you into trouble..."

"Alexandria, why do you fear being captured?" Dacia interrupted.

To this day I don't remember exactly why I feared getting into trouble, but I remember when I began fearing it—that was my wound. Still, I answered Dacia to the best of my ability.

"When I was little," I started. "I went with my mother to work on a Saturday. The office was almost completely deserted, but my mother had some work to catch up on. She told me I could wander around but not to touch anything. I found a section of the office that was under construction.

"I knew I shouldn't have gone in, but I did anyway. It was interesting to see everything half built. Somewhere in the middle of the area I found a cubicle that hadn't been completely cleaned out. Curious, I began looking at what had been left, wondering why it was still there." I lapsed into silence. The next part was what had scarred me.

"You were caught?" Zahi prompted.

I shook my head. "Someone came and I ran, they gave chase but I lost them and found my mother again, trying to pretend as if nothing had happened. I knew they had security cameras and I expected for the next several weeks to be arrested at any moment. I tried never to go to the office again if I could help it, and when I did I was careful to stay away from any and all people or cameras." I bit my lip. It was childish to think I could get arrested for simply wandering somewhere, it hadn't been trespassing, but I *was* a child.

The incident had haunted me. More so, apparently, than I'd realized, it had lodged itself deep in my soul. Some fears can remain buried like that and never go away, no matter how irrational or inane.

Dacia rode up closer to me and smiled understandingly. "It is all right, Alexandria," she said. "Now that you know how deep this fear goes, and what caused it, you can begin to heal."

δ

Chapter 4

That night, Dacia gave me my healer rite and cleansing. I revisited my original wound, now knowing what it was, and concentrated on understanding where it came from. When I stopped meditating and the rite was given, I felt whole in my soul again. I had been fragmented by the trauma and now that fragment had been returned.

Dacia told me that fear had hindered me all my life and as such my first chakra, located at the base of the spine, had been out of sync with the rest of my energy chakras. This block had stopped my emotional development at the age of the trauma. It explained why when under extreme negative pressure, I reverted to the emotional maturity of a young child.

Now that I understood, I could heal. With the healer rite my soul was whole again.

By morning we were out of the factory district, but still in the lower realm. When I asked Zahi about the realms he responded there were two realms below the one where we lived, considered the lower realms and there were upper realms too.

Which of the two lower realms we were currently in I did not know, and no one seemed particularly bothered with telling me. Looking around me, it was strange to think this world wasn't the one where I was born. Yet if I looked hard enough, I could see the differences. The colors were duller, and the sounds muffled. All of my senses seemed to be straining to detect all that they usually could, because all the usual information simply did not exist. Everything had a distinct flatness to it.

We passed trickling streams and still lakes, rough forests and flat paths but there were no mountains, or hills, just level terrain for as far as the eye could see.

Whenever we stopped for the night, Dacia would ask me about my life and we would do yoga, stretching to ease our bodies from travel and breathing in time to align our movement to the earth.

Over the firelight we would talk for hours and hours about who I was, what I wanted, what I believed in and go through the sun salutation. At first it made me uneasy to spill all my secrets and personal details out so casually. But over time, I understood it was meant to help me open up and leave the past behind me. The next step in whatever process Dacia had laid out for me was sense of the true self. Whatever we were to do next, I had to know who I was, what I stood for, and my purpose in the universe. The yoga helped with that; it connected my mind to my body and gave me a sense of oneness with myself and with the Universe.

Often I would find myself lost in thought, wondering what we could possibly be doing next that required me to have such a strong resolve.

What came next, however, I'm not sure I would have ever imagined.

{[][][][][][]}

Traumatic events can rip a soul, can render some part of yourself frozen or broken—banished to the lower worlds for safety. In the warehouse I had found that part of my soul. I had made myself whole and therefore could learn and heal. My sense of true self was altered by this encounter. It was awakened. The gaping fear I had grown used to no longer gripped me, and that took some time to get used to.

After several days measured only by the path of the sun, we came upon a small village. As we approached, a woman with beige clothes and dark hair wrapped in a bun on the top of her head appeared from seemingly nowhere, commanding our attention like a beacon.

"This village is not the place you seek," she said, sweeping her arms out in a peace making gesture. "I suggest you keep traveling."

Dacia nodded and signaled for us to turn aside and circumscribe the village.

"I don't understand," I whispered to Zahi as we began making our way around the village. "Why can't we go through?"

Zahi bit his lip as if trying to find the best way to explain something. "In the spiritual realms, there is a gatekeeper. Someone to reside over the lands and keep everyone on the path they are meant to take.

Some lessons are meant to be learnt in a specific order."

"Why?"

"Well, think of it like math. You have to learn to subtract before you can divide, you have to learn to divide numbers before you can divide polynomials. Some lessons just make more sense in one order than in another because they build upon each other. The gatekeeper exists to make sure that order is followed."

"Does that mean we'll come back to this village someday?" I wondered.

Zahi shrugged. "I don't know. Roads do wind back but life is full of twists and turns. Every decision changing the path that lies ahead, every thought forming ourselves. The road may wind back, but it may not lead to the same places it used to. We absorb so much information, every day, every hour, every minute. There is so much we learn that we hardly retain any of it for long."

"That's not true."

"Is it not? The things you remember, you remember because they have for some reason imprinted on your subconscious. Maybe it filled you so strongly with an emotion that it couldn't help but leave a mark. But most things we remember because they are repetitive—they happen all the time. Why do we all know that the sun rises and sets? Because it happens every day, without fail. We've learned and we've remembered because it is always there. That is what memory is like. The things we remember the most, we remember because they are always there for us."

As I thought about that, I looked up at the trees that lined the path. Their branches arched over our heads like a bridge, the dappled light glinting on the pebble-strewn dirt below. Meanwhile, the air was still, like it was holding its breath, an oppressive, nerve-wracking, yet mystical effect.

"Why does nothing move?" I asked after a time. It was starting to freak me out.

Dacia raised her eyebrows, "What do you mean, Alexandria?"

"The stillness of the path, of the trees, the lack of life, does it not bother you?"

"These trees embody life do they not?"

I shook my head exasperatedly. "You know that's not what I mean. Where are the birds? The squirrels? The bugs, even? There is life beyond plants, there are entire ecosystems that should be apparent."

"Why should the stillness upset you?" Dacia inquired, apparently at ease.

My agitation began to show. My fingers began to wiggle as if to grasp something but there was nothing to hold but the reins and Ace's black mane. "Life shouldn't be still. Even in peace, the wind blows, the world spins. Stillness is unnatural, its unhealthy..." I trailed off, at a loss for what I was trying to say.

Zahi spoke up, "In our dimension stillness is feared, and so portrayed as sinister. In this dimension the stillness is quite normal, a reflection of the world above. This land is but a shadow of ours to our eyes."

I thought on that for a bit then muttered, "It's still unnerving."

Dacia narrowed her eyes a bit then said in a thoughtful tone, "What frightens you, Alexandria?"

"Loneliness," I answered almost automatically. "Spiders, snakes. Losing someone I care about... I fear having absolutely no control over anything. I fear not being strong enough to do what's needed in scary situations. I fear the dark for what it can hide. I fear ignorance and the power it holds—"

"A bold and thoughtful list but you are answering more philosophically then I wish to know. What do you fear that is illogical, that holds no threat to your well-being?"

"If I fear something, I fear it because I think it will harm or control me. Whether or not you agree that it will harm or control me is another matter entirely."

The corner of Dacia's lip twitched up in an almost-smile. "What do you fear then, Alexandria, that is not a fear shared by everyone?"

"What do you mean?"

"Everyone fears losing a loved one. Everyone fears not being able to protect themselves or those they love in times of crisis. Everyone fears being alone, having no one. What do you fear that could be considered unique to you? Snakes, spiders, what else? You seem to fear the stillness, and the dark..."

Dacia trailed off, waiting for me to finish her sentence.

I thought carefully before answering. It really wasn't as easy a question as I had originally thought, and I didn't want to answer carelessly. I had a feeling that a lot depended upon my answer.

"I fear letting people down" I finally said, but then I corrected myself, "No, I fear that people will think less of me for failing to do what is asked of me. I want people to think highly of me, and I fear that they don't."

"What does it matter what other people think?" Zahi asked.

"It doesn't," I shrugged. "Not for my mental health at least. But it unfortunately matters a great deal in life. How others perceive me affects what jobs I get, what schools I go to. It affects who talks to me and what they say. Whether or not I care what people think of me does not change the fact that it sometimes matters very much how I am perceived."

"I'd never thought about it like that," Zahi said, looking thoughtful. "I've spent so much time away from it all, it's almost like I see our dimension through a film screen, distant and apart from myself."

"Alexandria, fear is a crippling thing. You have already shown that you can disregard fear for your own life in favor of saving someone else. But to truly understand yourself, you must be able to recognize all of your fears so they can be put aside when necessary. You fear the stillness of this wood. You fear it because you have been taught to fear inactivity. You fear it because you're afraid that there is something poised to pounce and you would not know because it makes no sound. You are so used to the rustle of the bustling world you grew up in that you interpret the silence as a death sentence to your perceived awareness.

"The unknown is always silent, Alexandria. There is always a surprise around the bend. Whether it strikes or remains in the shadows is a game of chance. There is no point in fearing the future. You will gain nothing from such an exercise."

{[][][][]}

As we traveled, I began to think we must be heading south. I hadn't bothered to look at the moss on the trees or to discern the stars high above in the inky sky where they hung like beacons, but the chill in the air was becoming decidedly more pronounced.

When I began to shiver, Zahi threw me a coat, and we continued—the temperature dropping with every hour. It's possible we were going north, if we'd traveled above the equator. I did not know the geography of this realm. Did it match ours? Was it different? Maybe west made it colder or perhaps the entire realm was trapped in the same biome and the seasons were just changing.

I made a mental note to ask Dacia at the next opportunity and looked around at the snow that had begun to dot the landscape. Either the last snowfall had been minimal, or most of it had melted, because grass and leaves poked up through the sparse white covering with frequency giving the land a dusted look.

The next village we came to was dusted with the same beautiful effect. The roofs were perfectly blanketed with the white snow, while the snow on the ground was torn up with boot marks, tire treads, and hoof prints. It reminded me of the villages in Christmas movies, especially when night fell and the lights of the houses shone bright through the town, casting their yellow lights onto the snow until it glimmered.

When I asked Dacia how long we would stay in the village she just shrugged, "However long we need to, Alexandria."

I rolled my eyes and turned to Zahi. "That means long enough that you should unpack," he said. I nodded; that was helpful information. I unzipped my bag and began moving into the empty dwelling. It was bigger than the last, instead of one room with corners designated to kitchen, bedroom, sitting room, and storage like the hut, this dwelling had three bedrooms, a fully functional kitchen, running water, electricity, and a family room.

My bedroom was very similar to the other two with hardwood floors, a round rug by the bed, a wardrobe in the corner, and a nightstand with a lamp next to the headboard. It took very little time to hang up the few clothes I had with me in the wardrobe. There hadn't been many opportunities the past few weeks to wash the clothing effectively, and some of it was starting to smell a bit rank. With luck there was a washing machine in this town.

I sat on the flower print bedspread and kicked the now empty bag under it. Around the house, I could hear Dacia and Zahi bustling about with the man who'd shown us to the house. He was a middle-aged man, sturdily built with peppery hair and a beard that could use a trim. He'd handed Dacia the keys and been in very good spirits as he listed all the features of the house. Most of it made no sense to me, he discussed the heat system, how the water worked, where to get food. He lost me at the breakers. I knew they controlled the electricity and if you turned one off the power went out. To me that was a perfectly satisfactory knowledge.

I didn't think the man had anything left to talk about, but they were discussing something animatedly in the family room. I turned to the bedside table and noticed there was a clock. It was the first time I'd seen the time since arriving at the train station. With some uneasiness I realized I did not know the date. Did time even pass the same in this realm? The clock didn't say it was lunchtime, but hunger gnawed at my stomach all the same.

The kitchen was fully stocked for our arrival and I'd just finished my sandwich when Zahi and Dacia came in.

"Come along, Alexandria. We've much to do."

"Where are we going?"

"To help."

{[|][|][|][|]}

Turns out we were the community service brigade. At least that's what I called it. That first day, we cleaned the local park, picking up trash, raking the leaves where the snow was melted enough to allow it, cleaning the equipment and repainting it. When new snow rendered the roads unusable, we shoveled them, throwing down salt and pushing the snow off to the side, doing our best to break up the ice.

Slowly, we began to integrate into the community. Dacia sent Zahi and I to the local school, which seemed to only teach our least favorite subjects. When I asked Dacia about it he simply replied, "Lower realms are reflections of human sufferings."

I guess that meant we could only learn the subjects that caused suffering as they were the only ones reflected across the realm divide. Didn't that just go figure.

We kept our horses at a barn on the outskirts of the city and Zahi and I rode in their arena as often as we could. I loved spending time with Ace and Fadia. It helped us stay grounded as we acclimated to the inconsistencies of the town.

There was one man, that we saw almost every day, who just emanated bad vibes. His slicked back hair was never out of place, his suits were always dark or pinstriped and fresh pressed daily, and his ties were perfectly ironed. He would walk down the streets and greet everyone by name, encouraging them to come to his shop.

I went there once. Everything had a place and everything was pristine. Unlike the rest of the realm which was dull and muffled his shop always seemed sharp. Sounds were still more muffled than I was used to, but the color brown popped with alarming intensity and the smell of fresh pine assaulted my nostrils.

The unctuous man was just finishing up with a customer, selling an old lady a nice little table for quite an exorbitant price. As she left, I watched him carefully because he hadn't gone back to his work; he was staring at her—watching her closely as she maneuvered through the shop with the table. Suddenly, he flicked his finger at something and went back to his work. I looked at the old lady just in time to see her trip over a low rise in the floor that I swear hadn't been there before, and drop the table.

"Oh dear," the man said, coming over to look. One of the table legs had splintered slightly and was now neither pleasing to look at or particularly sturdy. "Well, I can't let you go home with that, madam. How about I keep it here a little while and fix it up for you and deliver it to your house when I've finished?" The old lady thanked him profusely and he rang her up for the repair charges while I stalked out of the shop. I'd seen enough to know that the man was a right old crook. Whatever he had flicked had raised that floor and now he was taking advantage of the poor woman's plight and charging her more money!

Dacia would hear of this.

ℰ

Chapter 5

The dark of the sky and the dark of my mood made dinner a very gloomy affair. When I told Dacia of the crooked man she said that happens in life. When I'd insisted that we should do something—that we should help like we help other things—she'd told me now wasn't the time. The crooked man was beloved by society. To turn against him in the current state of things would mean our removal from the town. The people would have to realize his crooked nature on their own before they were ready to fix the problem.

While I understood her point, it frustrated me to watch this man rise through the ranks of society, loved by the people while being so slimy, I'm surprised he didn't sleep with slugs. With every passing day he made more money and won over more people with his generous facade. He would donate hundreds of dollars to charity and then run a festival in their honor, pocketing the entrance fee that he set.

"Why do the people not see him as we do?" I asked Zahi one day as we rode.

"They don't look as closely. To them, he is his facade. They see generosity all the way down to his core."

"Surely they realize that's foolish. Every person has at least two sides to them. I wonder what he's like when he's angry."

"Alexandria, you can't go terrorizing the man."

"I didn't say I would, I just said I was thinking about it."

"Well, trust me when I say that would cause more trouble than its worth."

I pursed my lips, but I didn't bring up the subject again.

{[][][][][]}

Election time brought on the real fiasco. Greasy man decided to run for mayor of the town. As the day approached, the town was bedecked in the red and blue flags of the opposing candidates. Slogans ran across street lamps, and little signs littered the grass, stuck in at odd angles and swaying in the breeze. The votes went in and greasy man won in a landslide. Slowly, the aura of the town began to change and Zahi, Dacia, and I found more work.

Funding for the city clean up initiative was cut, so we found ourselves picking up trash on the roadside, taking the trash from local businesses to the dump and their recyclables to the recycling plant to subsidize the government programs that suddenly couldn't afford it. Funding for the city pool was cut and we found ourselves repainting, re-caulking, refilling, and maintaining the pool in preparation for its opening in the summer as well as raising money to pay for and train lifeguards.

Taxes went up and rent quickly followed. The nice man that lent us our place had his main home taken by the bank after the renters he shared it with left, taking the money for the mortgage with them. So, Zahi was kicked out onto the couch and the nice man took his bedroom.

The school didn't have money for more paper, so recycling old paper became a big initiative in the community as well as printing in smaller and smaller fonts. By summer I was surprised we hadn't all gone blind from eye strain.

Even the city jail was affected as nutrition and rehab programs were cut. We ran food drives and fundraisers to feed the prisoners the balanced diet they needed to stay healthy, and to hire psychiatrists to help those that needed help. But sometimes, it still wasn't enough.

Nothing we did was enough on our own and so the mayor "helped" us fix all of the problems that arose by giving us his "full support."

No one bothered to notice that it was his budget cuts that were causing the problems, or that his tax increases to stop those budget cuts didn't seem to be getting the budget back at all.

I wanted to know how much he was pocketing, but knew better than to ask. Hard as it was, we were leading most of the efforts to help the people. If I dissed the beloved mayor, the nice man would kick us out and we wouldn't be able to afford to stay to help.

It was a frustrating balance, one I couldn't discover how to tip in the people' favor.

{[][][][]}

I'm not sure when the change began. By the time anyone noticed the change, we were so far in that it couldn't be avoided.

Isn't it strange how that happens? How something can begin so gradually you don't notice until the beginning can no longer be discerned amongst the haze of the past? You see it all the time with war. What began it? Historians tend date the start of a war as the date when the fighting broke out. But wars begin much earlier than that. They begin when the first person begins to feel dislike, jealousy, or spite towards whomever they end up fighting. The ego takes over and war follows.

When the majority of a nation's people share these attitudes, that's when the fighting begins, and that's when the historians document the war beginning. But World War II didn't really start with the invasion of Poland or Hitler rising to power in Germany. World War II began when the Allied

Powers crippled Germany economically at the end of World War I.

The war of the town, with the people on one side and the mayor on the other, began just like all wars. Zahi and I were the first to wage war on him. And then somehow, gradually, the people began to realize their mayor was corrupt. They became self-aware and started helping us to fight against him. People began grumbling under their breaths, then protests began to break out. Then the news story broke that the man had indeed been raising taxes and keeping the higher income to himself.

The war had begun and I planned to be on the front line right there with the people.

{[|][|][|][|]}

This being a lower realm, I guess things escalated towards suffering a lot quicker than in our realm, or things just went faster in general. At any rate it seemed like I'd barely blinked after the news story broke before the people were dragging the mayor down the street to the court house, pelting him with tomatoes and chasing him with torches and pitchforks. I didn't even know people did that anymore.

The mayor was going to be held accountable for his actions the papers said. The trials went on for days, with witness after witness testifying. Zahi, Dacia, and I ignored the uproar. Dacia said I'd helped spark the fire enough, I should let the people decide his fate for themselves. I didn't really feel like I'd done anything, but I listened to her advice as always.

And so we went about our usual business; picking up trash and repainting what needed a fresh coat. We were painting the street lamps when the verdict was reached. Death penalty.

I looked at Zahi and Dacia in surprise. "Death penalty seems a bit extreme don't you think?" I asked, my eyebrows furrowed. My dark hair was pulled back in a ponytail like it always was when I worked, but several strands had fallen out and I struggled to get them out of my face without painting them as I waited for their answer.

"It does seem extreme," Dacia finally said, "but this is not our society, Alexandria, it is how they do things here."

"It just doesn't seem right to kill him though. Yes, he's a bad guy and the homeless population has increased significantly since he took office, but death? Really?"

"It is what the courts decided, though there is always an appeal. Perhaps we could go to that and make your sentiments known," Dacia offered.

"I thought we weren't to interfere in politics," I muttered grumpily.

"This man's cover is blown. He won't be trusted by this town again, and you're right, the death penalty is extreme. Even in this case."

"But if I stand up for him won't the town just turn against me? I mean that's why we couldn't condemn him in the first place."

"Times are different now, Alexandria, than when we first arrived," Dacia began. "When we arrived we were new. We were welcome, but we certainly weren't appreciated. To stand against the populace then would have meant ostracism. Now we are one of them, and we can appeal to their humanity like we never could have appealed to the mayor's."

"Are you saying the mayor is not human?" Zahi interrupted.

Dacia sighed. "I said we could not appeal to his humanity. There is a difference.

His morals are not ours. He made that clear when he was robbing the people. Therefore, we could never force him to see the light. And it would have taken too long to show him the light, especially when he had no desire to see it. The people know the morals of which we will speak, even if they are lost. All we have to do is remind them of their consciences. And that, my friends, is a much easier task."

So that is how we ended up at the appeal of greasy Mr. Mayor to save his life. Though we had a feeling he wouldn't have returned the favor if our situations were reversed.

{[I][I][I][I][I]}

The appeal was a nightmare. The entire town shouting at once; their points lost in the din until the courtroom was a babble of incensed chaos. The gavel banged for silence, adding to the cacophony with its useless wooden sound that nobody heard but those close enough to see it fall. However, as the message of the banging gravel traveled, silence spread like a ripple until a pin could be dropped and heard.

The mahogany furniture of the courtroom threatened to break under the weight of the people as they crammed in to hear the proceedings, while outside the courthouse the rest of the town waited with bated breath.

It was such a spectacle I'm surprised they didn't put it in a stadium.

The lawyers sat next to the former mayor, whose greased hair was sticking up at odd angles. His suit had creases in it, and there were large dark circles under his eyes. I wondered how he felt to have climbed so far up only to fall back down lower than he'd started.

"We are all here today to review the death penalty of one whom has wronged us all," the judge began in his slow cracking voice. "Under his charge, the homeless rate has increased 20%, taxes were raised 60%, budgets were cut 70% and our mayor kept all extra funds for his own personal gain."

The crowd booed the former mayor with venom in their breaths. Oh how the tide had turned. I almost felt sorry for the man. Almost.

"Now under these charges this man has been sentenced to death. Are there any here who would dispute that sentence?"

I looked around. No one else had stood, not even Zahi and Dacia, but I had. I'd stood without even thinking about it. I looked down at Zahi and Dacia questioningly. Did they not agree with me? But Dacia gave me a small nod and I understood. They both agreed with me, but they wanted me to fix it. It was my battle to win and they were letting me, standing by to help if it got out of hand.

"Alexandria, do you not realize what this man has done?" The judge asked me, his very tone urging me to sit down and stop being foolish.

"I do your honor," I said, standing up taller. "I understand what he has done."

"Do you not agree he needs to be punished?"

"I do agree he must be punished."

"Then why, my dear, are you standing?" The judge asked me, his aggravation barely contained beneath the thin veneer of his smile and condescending tone.

"I do not agree that the punishment for his crimes should be death. I do not think his crimes extreme enough to warrant such forceful action."

The uproar this caused was ridiculous. The entire town began yelling at once, directing their anger at any available subject, with a fair amount getting sent directly at me. Only Zahi and Dacia remained silent, supporting me, one on each side of me, nodding when I looked down, encouraging me to keep going. The judge banged his gavel down repeatedly shouting "order" as if it would make a difference. Through the cacophony I stood, holding my head high and waiting for the townspeople to settle down, I knew they would, it was just a matter of time. They'd get their anger out. They'd realize that it was getting them nowhere.

It seemed like an eternity before order was re-established, but once most of the townspeople had run out of things to say, I began the speech I'd been running through my head since the minute I'd heard about the death sentence.

"Hear me out!" I cried, silencing the rest of the shouts. "This man has committed exorbitant crimes, I agree. But not one of his crimes has taken a life. He has destroyed lives, sure. But, he has not caused the death of any one of you. Why then, are we going to commit such a crime against him. Why should we take his life when he has taken none of ours? What example does this set for the children? What sort of role models are we if our punishments are harsher than the crime committed? Would you encourage your children to punch their enemies because they took their cookie? Or would you encourage them to tell an adult so that adult can punish the child by taking away their sweets, or grounding them. This man has taken money that is not his and used it for his own personal gain putting some of you into desperate situations.

"I say we do the same to him. How much money did he steal? Take it back. Put it back in the city budget. Give money to the schools, to the city. Give them the money that they have been starved of since he took office. You all know his character. Will you ever trust him again?"

"No!" They shouted back with force.

"Then how is he to get a job? He'll have to live on his savings, like many of you who were laid off after budget cuts. He will reap what he has sown and he shall perhaps learn the error of his ways. But he shouldn't be killed."

Dacia smiled at me, standing up before the floor was lost.

"My pupil speaks true and you would do well to listen to her. Do not let your hearts harden against violence because of the errors of this man. Remember the people you are, the helpful people who care for the well-being of this town. Remember, and stand with us. We will not let this man go to his death."

I will never forget the miracle of that day. When I turned a village back to peace, or at least away from murder. The image of a majority of the townspeople standing for the crook filled me with a hope I could hardly explain. Humanity wasn't lost. Not even in this realm of shadows.

People with bad intentions and faulty morals exist everywhere. But if we stoop to their level and dole out punishments that are undeserved are we any better? That town that day did the right thing, and we all felt better for it; the crooked mayor was sent to jail for five years and all the funds he had stolen were put back into the budget and—through restoring the budgets that had been cut—given to the people.

{[|][|][|][|]}

"Well done today, Alexandria," Dacia told me at dinner. We ate out, a special occasion for it was the first time we had ever gone out to a restaurant since I'd joined the "school."

"It is not easy to stand alone," she continued, "it takes a great deal of courage and resolve to stand against a tide of anger. You did well."

I smiled, it was nice to be complimented. But I knew Dacia and Zahi could have done just as good a job as I— perhaps even better. They had been at this longer after all.

"It was fun to watch," Zahi said. "I never knew how powerful it looks to stand alone. It's always been something that I've done because it's right. But I must say it also looks mighty impressive. I think those people stood with you more because they were impressed with your courage more so than they agreed with you."

"Well, they stood all the same, so we must be thankful for that," Dacia mediated.

"I think we did get through to them, even if just a bit. I saw more than one person hang their head in shame as I spoke. It felt weird though, like I had power over them. But I have no power in this town. I'm just a girl that helps out."

"It takes a leader to lead, Alexandria, but that leader need not have a title," Dacia responded.

Zahi and I looked at each other. I wasn't entirely sure what Dacia meant at the time, but by now I think I've figured it out.

Just because one doesn't have a title of leadership—mayor, president, king—doesn't mean that one isn't a leader. Leadership is an aspect of personality; it's the ability to take charge of a situation when necessary. That day I had been a leader in the community because I stood up; Dacia was always a leader to us; and Zahi often took the lead when we went riding as he had a better sense of direction.

That night, when we went back to the house, I began packing up my things again. I had a feeling that our time in this village had come to a close. Tomorrow we would be off to new places, new adventures, and new lessons. I'd learned how important it is to know who you are and what you stand for. It was time to move on.

Sometimes you'll find yourself standing alone and that can be frightening, but if you are secure in who you are then you'll come out all the stronger for it because you will know that you did your best. And that is all anybody can ever ask of your true self.

Chapter 5

Chapter 6

The next night we moved again, just as I thought we would. The clouds covered the stars so we travelled in near darkness; the only light coming from two small lanterns that lit two feet of ground in front for the horses to see. At some point the fog rolled in, the damp began seeping through my clothing and dimming the lantern lights.

I wanted to ask where we were going, but I knew I wouldn't get a straight answer. Dacia never told us anything she didn't think we needed to know without questions; she was an enigma. It suddenly occurred to me that I probably shouldn't trust her, but I shrugged off the feeling; it was a little late to be thinking like that now.

The next thing I was aware of was soot and ash replacing the damp, fresh air and clogging my throat. Dimly, between the coughs that racked my system I could hear Zahi coughing equally as violently.

"Quiet you two," Dacia snapped immediately shutting us up. It was the first time either of us had heard Dacia angry and so we suppressed the coughs, straining our lungs to bursting. "We're back in our world," she continued. "The shades of ego here are much harder to find."

Whatever that meant. I think I knew though, the shades of the ego were the characteristics—anger, jealousy, greed, envy —that were mirrored into the lower realm. In the lower realms they were easy to find, easy to identify because they were the only thing mirrored; the only strong emotions found. All the other pleasant or desirable emotions were dull, muted, and not easily identified. Happiness could be elation or love or peace and you wouldn't be able to tell the difference.

In this realm, the one I knew best, the one where I grew up, all the emotions were mixed together. It would be more difficult to pick out the ego.

At least that's what I think she meant.

I didn't know where we were, but it was a far cry from the outback—the last place we'd seen in this realm, before traveling to the lower realm. The small street was heavily populated and dirtier than a back alley. The people stumbled about as if asleep, not taking notice of the horses that walked through their midst or their miserable surroundings they'd grown accustomed to.

The tallest building in the district rose up before us, rising out of the ground as if it had come from it. As I stared at its imposing stature I was forced to shield my eyes as the last few rays of daylight reflected off the windows, temporarily blinding me.

"Keep your eyes shut, Alexandria," came Dacia's voice.

"Why?" I asked, naturally curious. It didn't seem the safest environment to go around blind.

"Tell me what you see."

"My eyes are shut."

"Don't use your eyes. This is your world, even if it's not where you lived in it. Tell me what you can see."

I huffed and tried to focus on what I could hear. The hooves clopped on the concrete surface and the rush of people around was cacophonous—vendors shouting their wares on street corners, tavern owners throwing out the rabble-rousers. I heard it all as a jumble when my eyes were open. It was just noise; I didn't pay it any attention. But with my eyes shut, the noises became clear. It wasn't a jumble; it was individuals; it was a story. All of it going on inside my head, all at once, just little snippets, pieces of conversations.

The quality of the noises changed as Ace lurched forward slightly. We had stepped off of a curb; I could feel it. Instead of the sharp sound of hooves on the sidewalk I heard the dull muted shuffling of the horses walking over grass. Instead of bike horns and angry yelling I heard children screaming, playing games. Instinctively I ducked and opened my eyes just in time to see a frisbee go sailing right where my head had been.

Zahi caught it with ease and threw it back, smirking slightly.

"See this is why we don't close our eyes whilst walking," I complained to Dacia. "You could get hurt."

"How did you know to duck, Alexandria?"

I shrugged.

I had ducked and opened my eyes before acknowledging I was even performing those actions.

"You knew," Dacia asserted. "I brought you back to this plane of the universe to practice sensing. Seeing without your eyes. Perhaps you will learn better in the level you came from. You are more used to it."

I had no idea what Dacia was talking about but it sort of made sense.

Our dwelling this time was a small condo somewhere between the industrial district and the more upscale city. As we settled in, I sat on the bed's colorful geometric quilt and closed my eyes. I could hear the hum of the fridge downstairs, the creak of the wood and the thump of footsteps as Zahi and Dacia walked about. The air conditioning kicked on, making the whole house vibrate gently as it pushed through the ducts. It was surprising how noisy the world was when you closed your eyes.

I could smell the musty lemon of old wood from the furniture in the room and the dusty mothball scent that clung to the blankets and pillows. The carpet beneath my feet was worn but still cushioning. With a sigh I fell backwards onto the twin bed, flinching as the wood creaked and moaned. Dacia assured me it wouldn't break but the sounds still bothered me. They didn't sound safe.

Somewhere outside a dog barked. I looked towards the one window in the room —it could've used some curtains—and watched the late afternoon sunlight blaze into the room alighting the dust particles as they drifted aimlessly about, dancing in the beams. I should get a dog.

"Alexandria," Zahi called.

"In my bedroom." The door was still open and as Zahi rounded the corner of the staircase outside I could see he was holding something. "What's that?"

"A blindfold."

"Why do you have a blindfold?"

"Dacia wants you to wear it."

"Um. No."

Zahi rolled his eyes. "She says it will help develop your sensing if you can't be tempted to use your eyes."

"So why don't you have to wear one?"

Zahi pursed his lips. "I do," he grumbled shoving the piece of black cloth at me and pulling out an identical length from his back pocket.

"What are the odds we're going to fall down the stairs?"

"Extreme. Together?"

"Together."

I put the black cloth up to my eyes—tied it around my head—and the world went pitch black. I couldn't see anything, not even the vague lightening effect you'd get if you just closed your eyes and looked towards a lamp or the sun.

It was going to be a long day.

{[|][|][|][|]}

After a while it was obvious why Dacia had insisted on the blindfold. Every time I ran into something I opened my eyes and got annoyed when it was unproductive. The scratchy blindfold made me use my other senses—touch, smell, hearing—to deduce what I'd run into. For the most part that meant furniture though once I ran into something and, reaching down to figure out what, I'd realized two things: one, I had somehow managed to get outside and two, what I'd run into was no longer in front of me so it had probably been alive. I was glad there was a fence around the property. It wouldn't be fun to get accidentally run over.

After the fifth time I ran into a wall and smashed my nose, I had wanted to rip the blindfold off my head and flush it down the toilet. Dacia must have known because she told me not to take it off.

Once I'd figured out the layout of the house, the blindfold was no longer a hindrance, simply a nuisance. Zahi told me it was like wandering around without his glasses on. He could manage just fine, but between the blurriness of his surroundings and the inability to read anything without being so close it touched his nose, it irked him to no end.

I think the blindfold was easier than bad eyesight. At least with the blindfold you didn't have any clear idea of what you were missing, wandering about with poor vision you'd be able to see enough to know what details you missed.

After about a week I was so used to the blindfold I could even cook a bit without burning myself (or anything else). The oven was still off limits as was the stove top and cooking meat, but I could use the microwave and the toaster relatively well.

The exercise was helping; much to my surprise. I could track Zahi and Dacia around the house simply by listening to the resonance of their footsteps. When the refrigerator broke I was the first to notice because the hum it made changed pitches.

When Zahi and I played board games, we didn't have to see. When we played checkers we listened for where the pieces stopped and memorized the board in our minds. I'm not sure someone with a poor memory could have adjusted to the dark the way Zahi and I did. Or perhaps it was because we had no other choice that we adjusted as we did.

During the first few days, Dacia had made a point of keeping us in her sights so we wouldn't remove the blindfolds and cheat. Now she was less concerned, but we were so used to them, we stopped wanting to.

"Why is it important for us to learn to use our senses?" I asked Dacia one day at lunch.

"You haven't figured that part out yet?" she asked mildly, taking a bite of her sandwich.

Zahi and I shook our heads, I could hear the swish caused by the shift in clothing.

"Each realm we travel too has different characteristics. Alexandria, you recognized the stillness and the muted nature of the dimension adjacent to this one on the lower planes."

I nodded.

"How do you think we were able to access that world? How do you think we travelled?"

That was a difficult question. We'd been on our horses, but I'm not sure that was completely relevant. We'd been in the middle of nowhere, but when we'd come back it had been right in the middle of the industrial section.

"I'm not sure," I finally responded. "I've only done it twice and I wasn't paying enough attention either time."

Dacia nodded but I could sense her disapproval.

"The rifts are hidden well. And the mindset must be right," Zahi cut in.

"That is true, Zahi, but that does not answer Alexandria's question."

"If the rifts are gateways, and they are hidden, does being able to sense your surroundings well allow you to find them?" I asked.

"Now you two are getting somewhere," Dacia said approvingly as she sipped some of her soup.

That lifted a weight from my shoulders. Disappointing Dacia always made me feel inferior. I wanted to be worthy of this incredible experience she had given me.

Just then the doorbell rang. I should've known something was wrong as soon as it did. We never got visitors, packages were never delivered until dinnertime, and it wasn't like the mailman rang the doorbell.

"I'll get it." Zahi jumped up and ran to the door, intercepting the man just as he had turned to go. He had a letter for Dacia. The letter that changed everything.

{[|][|][|][|]}

"I have to leave. You two will be fine. Zahi is eighteen now, he's in charge. Start attending the community college in town until I get back, I took the liberty of enrolling you for the semester. If I'm not back by then enroll yourselves in the next semester."

"But where are you going?" I asked again. It wasn't like Dacia to just get up and leave. We had so much more to learn.

"There are urgent matters that need my help."

"Let us come with you! That's what you've been teaching us to do: help!" Zahi insisted.

"You two do not yet have the training required to help in this particular case. And don't go trying to help anything extraordinary here either. Some situations are too big, and you don't know the difference yet."

"Well what *are* we supposed to do?!" Zahi practically shouted.

Dacia gave him a withering look.

"Sorry," Zahi muttered.

"Volunteer in town if you must. Keep up with your studies. Remember what I've taught you and remember who you are. Keep meditating and continue practicing Yoga daily. Sun salutation is a brilliant way to focus the mind and body to the energy of the world. You can take the blindfolds off, but do not forget to be aware of the world around you. Awareness is a key step to learning. Take care of the horses. Ride as often as you can." Dacia stepped out of the door and swung her bag onto her shoulder. "Stay safe, stay here," she said. And then she was gone.

"I can't believe she would just leave us here!" Zahi ranted.

I just felt numb. Dacia was our teacher, our mentor. We were lost without her guidance. Not to mention she was the only adult in our lives and I didn't think Zahi counted as a replacement. We didn't even know where we were. We hadn't been to town since we arrived here and nobody had bothered telling us what the town was called.

I'd be eighteen too come spring. Dacia had left us on our own like the future college students we were, but I don't think that was right. We weren't ready to be on our own. Not yet, anyway.

{[|][|][|][|]}

Our routine was simple, we'd get up in the morning and take the bus to the college. We were taking classes in non-profits and history with English and math on the side. Psychology was interesting, though it was the closest thing to a science we took. No one else really understood us, so we stuck together at lunch and between classes discussing our theories about what Dacia had been teaching us. Neither of us knew how many dimensions there were, or how to get to them. We did some research on the chakras and learned about them as much as we could, though it wasn't much help. After school we would volunteer at local organizations until suppertime when one of us would cook. After dinner we did our sun salutation and meditated and did our homework then put our blindfolds on until bed.

In this fashion, months went by. Soon it was winter and the wind picked up bringing with it icy roads and stormy skies.

Zahi was at his wits end with routine. He hadn't gone to school in half a decade besides those few months in the lower realm and by the first snowfall he'd stopped going to the college. He wanted something exciting to happen, something that was new. I told him he was crazy and I kept going to school, though I was lonely without him there.

Deep down, I wanted adventure too, though it was nice to be sleeping in a real bed for so long. The tents we stayed in while traveling got old quick as did the hard ground they rested on. But routine was boring and it was wearing on my soul.

Winter wore on and I began to feel the familiar isolation I'd felt in high school. It wasn't that the kids were mean to me, they just didn't even notice me. I was a ghost to them, a flicker of existence that attended classes then disappeared. Zahi and I had made our own little clique. When he stopped coming, I was alone. I started taking more classes, as many as I could to fill the empty spaces of my day. At first that was fine. Then I got overwhelmed. The homework began taking me all night, I began to skip volunteering to stay caught up. Twice a week I put off the mountains of reading and writing to visit Ace at the local stable. Being with her, spending time grooming her light brown coat and running the comb through her thick black mane, it kept me sane as did yoga the one time a week I managed to fit it in.

Weather permitting, I would always take Ace out in the arena and ride. There weren't any good trails about and I could sense her frustration at always going around the same circle. I apologized. There wasn't anything I could do to fix it though. I started taking her over some jumps again. I praised her mightily whenever she did something new well. These short few hours in the barn were a lifesaver. I was alone, but I wasn't isolated. Ace loved me and I loved Ace, and that saved me.

Getting up in the morning was getting harder. The alarm would go off and I would force my eyes open, trying to determine a reason, any reason that was a valid excuse for not getting up. I never could find one. I think I stopped ever waking up at all. I just went through the motions of life, one step at a time. I was no longer doing anything Dacia had told us too. I'd stopped researching the lessons she'd started. Zahi noticed, but when he tried to help me get back on track, I yelled at him. I could feel my life spiraling out of control, spiraling into the routine nothingness that high school had been. I just didn't have the time to do the stuff that I wanted to do. I was forced to spend all of my time doing schoolwork, pleasing authorities of a system that taught no valuable techniques; though some subject matter was occasionally helpful.

Everything was left-brain oriented. For my birthday Zahi bought me painting supplies. He remembered that I'd loved to paint, and he thought a right-brain activity would do me some good. It was one of the most heartfelt gifts I'd ever received.

By the end of the year I was ready to explode. I'd started blowing off my schoolwork to focus on Dacia's lessons with Zahi. As a result, my grades were slipping, my teachers were getting annoyed. I was trying to balance everything and it wasn't working. I needed a break, I needed to do something different.

Sometimes at night I could feel this overwhelming pressure growing in my chest, like a power that I had yet to explore. It reminded me of movies where characters with superpowers suddenly explode and shoot their element in every direction in frustration. I wanted to do that. I wanted to just fling away all the negative energy. But I'm not a superhero. I don't have powers. And the negative energy stayed welled up inside, driving me insane.

Perhaps that's why I let Zahi talk me into going to the protest. I wanted to feel as if I'd done something. I wanted to bring relief to the doldrums of society that plagued me.

Chapter 7

"Come on, Alexandria. It's our job to help. That's why we're here."

"Dacia told us to mind our own business when it came to the big issues! She said we were enough help volunteering."

"You've seen how the people in the industrial section are treated. We have to *do* something about it." Zahi insisted.

"We *are* doing something about it. We collect food and blankets and toiletries for them," I bit back.

"That's a poor way to help."

"It's all we can do! We're just kids, how are we supposed to help change things?"

"We can go help protest their treatment!"

"Zahi we're just kids, what if the police start shooting or something?"

"It's a peaceful protest. We're not doing anything against the law. Come on, half the college is going. They don't know the things we do and they help, so it must be okay. Just like it's okay for us to volunteer."

I couldn't argue against that point, but the whole thing still made me nervous. We went anyway.

We made signs and rode the bus down to the industrial area of town to join the protesters as they marched through main street. We wouldn't stop until the workers had their basic needs met. At least that was the idea. When the police had the firemen turn their hoses on us, chaos erupted. We'd made a huge mistake coming.

I remember hearing gunshots and dropping to the ground with Zahi. The firing ceased but the stampeding people didn't as they all rushed to get indoors, the police let them run, the protest had failed, they'd won. Some of the more desperate industrial workers were incensed. They stormed the police brigade at the end of the street and more shots began to ring through the tumultuous air.

"We have to get out of here Zahi!" I shouted and then I felt it. A dull patch in the air around us, just off to the side down an alley. It was like everything around it was being sucked in; an invisible vacuum. I knew it was a rift.

"Let's go!" I shouted, not even stopping to consider if it was a good idea to go world hopping or to remember what would happen when we descended lower. I should have remembered. So much would have been different had I remembered.

Together Zahi and I ran into the alley. I felt my stomach turn and suddenly we were in a different alley in a different realm, like a dream. We turned around in unison and screamed as a body came flying at us.

"Alexandria this is the lowest world!" Zahi managed to shout as a police man grabbed his arms and jerked them behind him.

I was freaking out. The lower worlds reflected all the bad of our own; how could I ever have though we'd be safe in them? The chaos was ten times as worse. The people didn't look quite human either. The few glimpses I caught of them as I was dragged down the street with Zahi showed me only warped images of people. They were twisted and changed by the realm we were in, the warped desires of human nature concentrated in one place. Or maybe my adrenaline was just pumping so fast I couldn't think or see straight.

Down here, I could sense all the hate and anger that had been building up in the industrial workers in my own world, the middle realm, because here it was not contained. It was dumping marbles down the stairs; noisy and un-retractable.

Everywhere I looked, violence reigned as people were shot, mutilated, and cut down on both sides of the fight. Zahi and I were dragged down the streets along with several other young participants and thrown into cells in the jailhouse. They weren't like the cells in the middle realm though, they were solid and dark and smelled of mold. There wasn't a single window, and no door that I could find. They were more like pits.

I was thrown down into one and I looked up in time to see Zahi be thrown down into one next door. The walls were too thick to hear him, but I prayed he was okay; it wasn't exactly a safe distance to fall.

The police left, and I was alone in my cell, in the dark, knowing this was all my fault.

There was a water tap in the side of the wall and the police threw food down at us at seemingly random intervals. Sometimes it felt like hours, other times it felt like days. And never once did I see another human being. I was alone, and it looked like I would be that way until I died. There was no justice in this realm and there was no escape.

{[|][|][|][|]}

I began to dream more vividly. Perhaps to make up for the darkness in which I lived. I couldn't remember the last time I'd seen the light. I missed Ace and the days we spent outside. I missed riding next to Zahi as he rode Fadia like it was the easiest thing in the world. I missed my parents and wondered if they were worried about me. I had kept in touch with them in the year that Dacia was gone. They'd wanted to come up for my birthday but couldn't afford it. I was secretly glad. I missed them terribly but my situation would have been too hard to explain.

I wondered if they'd find the funds now that I'd disappeared. Did time pass the same in all the dimensions? I hoped it didn't. I hoped time just paused, right where we'd left. It was easier to imagine that then to imagine their dismay and heartbreak.

My dreams took me back to my world in the middle realm. I would find myself in class again, taking a math test, or at home trying to get someplace, unable to see. My dreams put me in extraordinary positions. I could be a teacher of a preschool class, an amazing soccer player, a spy. In my dreams I was a goddess; everywhere and anywhere, a billion little me's spread across the Universe. I was infinite.

I think I began to sleep more hours than I was awake. I never really bothered to open my eyes except to eat. I knew every crack and crevice in the cell. I knew every sound, every smell, every texture.

One day, one of the soldiers dropped a nail down into the cell. It wasn't much use to get out, but it was something to do. The gentle scratching of the nail in the dirt was comforting. I drew pictures of mountains, of the sun. They reminded me of cave drawings, monochromatic and simple.

My thoughts strayed to Zahi. He was next door, supposedly. Aimlessly I began to scratch through the dirt of the wall between us. Perhaps I could dig through. Human contact would be a blessing after so long in the dark. Even just a single word. A single voice other than my own—something to tell me I wasn't alone. The only indication I had of that was the warden's boots as they walked across the observation deck above at irregular intervals. It wasn't much of a comfort.

My efforts were useless. There was a stone wall running under all that dirt. An immediate barrier to any interactions between the prisoners. I sank back, defeated. I should have known. It was silly to allow interactions. Interactions could lead to uprisings and escapes.

In my dreams, I looked for the light. I sought it with every molecule of my being. It had to be somewhere. I imagined myself on a grassy hill, basking in the late afternoon glow of the sun after a picnic. There weren't ever any bugs in my dreams, though my vision was often obscured. I was sensing in my dreams, not seeing. Often I couldn't even open my eyes.

The darkness was a great place for reflection, for memory. I was able to go through my entire life, one bit at a time, examine the moments, take them apart. I often found myself crying silently; wishing for the simple times of my childhood when the world was big but I was small and safe. I could barely remember some things; like the way it felt to be wrapped in a nice blanket, or the way it felt to lie on a pillow. The sun was a distant memory. Faces swam across my mind like ghosts, hazy and out of focus. But I knew who they were and they made me sad.

I began to compile all the mistakes I'd made, and all the good I'd done. I laid them out in front of me, scratching them into the dirt. I tried to search for some rhyme or reason as to their difference. What made the mistake different from the triumph?

Dark emotions coursed through me like shadows. Depression, anxiety, regret, self-deprecation, anger, they flit through me constantly, bringing with them more darkness. They were banished by the light: joy, peace, forgiveness, love, understanding. But the longer I was in the cell, the harder it was to remember the light. After a while I could only remember the bad things I'd done. The mistakes I'd made, the people I'd hurt.

I looked for the bright side everywhere but it was lost to me, floating beneath the surface of an opaque lake. My mind was too polluted to clean. I felt like a lost cause.

{[|][|][|][|]}

Time was a mirage. It had ceased to exist in my mind. All I knew was the pit. I sat in the corner, always in the same position, my knees tucked up against my chest, my head down on my arms. I'd given up on everything. There was nothing left to do but die. There was no way out of the dark and so I sat there, lost and alone, wasting away.

"What are you doing, Alexandria?" The familiar voice asked.

"I'm lost, Dacia. It's too dark."

"The light is never gone. Find it."

"I can't, I've tried."

"Try again."

Frustrated I screamed and threw the nail away. As I lifted my arm I noticed the dried blood. I'd been unconsciously using myself as a drawing board.

I was horrified. I stood up and fled the corner where I'd taken residence. I threw myself at the walls, struggling to climb out, to escape. I felt my blood coursing with darkness and tried to flee.

"Alexandria, calm down."

"I can't do this, Dacia. I'm losing my mind. I've lost everything," I sobbed.

The darkness loomed in on me, crushing me, it got into my throat and eyes, closing my airway, invading my mind.

"Alexandria. Think of Ace. Remember Zahi, your family. The sun as it sets over the water. The wind as it blows the clouds across the sky. The birds as they chirp, invisible in the trees, hailing the dawn of spring and the morning sun."

I was hyperventilating. "Ace," I breathed out, hugging myself with crushing strength. I tried to recall the color of her coat, the heat of her body, the warmth and peace of her presence. I tried to remember the sound of her nicker, the feel of her tongue as she took mints from my hand. I pictured Zahi, tall and strong helping me carry boxes to my room, appearing out of the darkness to show me the light. Ace was a light brown, her mane was dark. Zahi's coloring matched my horse's.

I smiled and laughed through my tears. I had never noticed that before. Laughter felt good. Laughter felt free. I strained my memory as images flashed across my mind.

Images of happiness, of laughter. My family at Christmastime, gathered around the tree singing carols. Riding Ace out in the fields, Fadia and Zahi by our side, running through nature like eagles, soaring side by side.

I remembered the first time I'd seen the ocean. The view off a mountain as the sun sinks beyond the horizon. The snow as it floats down gently from the sky, unhurried and relaxed. The rain as it brings life to new flowers.

Gradually, I felt myself calm down. I opened my eyes and squinted against a bright white light that hung in front of me.

"Dacia?" I asked.

"Hello, Alexandria."

I could make out her shape, haloed by the white light.

"How are you here?" I murmured.

"Who says I am?" she responded in her maddening way.

"I'm losing it, Dacia," I whispered.

"You're almost there, Alexandria."

"Where?"

"Freedom."

"From what?"

"This cell, the darkness that's held you all your life."

"You make it sound easy."

"Enlightenment is never easy."

"It's impossible to be truly enlightened."

Dacia smiled.

"It is true you will not come out of this knowing all there is to know. But you will be one step closer, Alexandria. The hardest step will be over. The sparkle of light will grow. Enlightenment is possible; it just takes work and practice."

I was silent, staring transfixed at the light.

"Keep following the light, Alexandria. You will make it out of here."

"There is no way out, Dacia. There is no light to follow."

"There is always light. Even in the darkest of places. You just have to know where to look, stay peaceful, and stay patient."

"How much longer, Dacia."

"As always it is up to you."

"What will be next?"

"Life."

The light disappeared and darkness enveloped me once more. Maybe I went to sleep, maybe I just stopped dreaming.

{[][][][]}

My next dream I had wings. I was soaring over the world as it unfolded beneath me, the yellow lights of cities sparkling like fallen stars forming the most beautiful map. As I flew out over the ocean, a wave came up to meet me, carrying me up towards the moon and the sky. Just before I reached them, however, the wave crashed against the shore, flinging me down into the spiraling abyss of water.

I plunged into the depths, and panic took me as I tried to right myself in the swirling darkness. I broke the surface and panic was replaced with serenity as I watched the sun break the horizon, rising up to take its rightful place in the sky.

I woke up with a resolution in my heart. It was time to leave. I got up and went to the water tap, turning it on and letting to cool water run across my hands. I couldn't remember the last time I'd bathed. My pale skin was practically black with grime. The dirt cell had rubbed off on me over time, and I wasn't sure I even looked human. The water cut through the grime, sending rivers of muck across the floor to pool in the corners.

The minuscule drain soon clogged with mud, and hair, and pieces of worn cloth that ripped off as I scrubbed. But I continued to run the water, rubbing it through my hair, across my face, and arms.

The water was colder than I would have ever used at home, but now the cold was welcome. It woke me from my stupor and brought reality ever closer. It brought memories of swimming with my siblings in the early days of summer before the sun had heated the newly opened pool.

As the grime washed away, the cell began to fill. Soon I was ankle deep in muck, but my pale arms stood out in the darkness, and I could see my hand in front of my face again. My wet hair fell in tangled knots down my back, and my wet clothes clung to me with alarming fervor. I wasn't sure they would ever be clean again.

And still the water kept going, filling up the cell with floating dirt. I wondered how far it would fill. I wondered if the dirt on the walls would mix with the water until the stone beyond held it in or if the dirt was too old, too packed to be affected by the slowly rising tide.

The more the water filled the cell, the less mucky it became. There just wasn't enough dirt to keep it sludge the whole twenty feet up.

Soon the water was too deep to stand, but too shallow to reach my bars and so I began to tread to keep my mouth above the surface. My muscles began to burn, one of my feet cramped up but still I swam about. It felt good to be doing something for once, instead of sitting in one place. I kept swimming until I could reach the bars. I hadn't really added them into my plan. I wasn't quite tiny enough to fit through them.

"Help!" I yelled. I didn't want to have to try and go find the tap in the murky water and turn it off. I wanted out. "Help!" I yelled again. I had to pull my face closer to the bars to breathe as the water kept filling the pit up.

Desperately I tried to remember when the warden had last walked by. I couldn't figure it out. Surely he had to come by soon though.

It was getting harder and harder to breathe. I'd have to go find the tap soon or I'd drown. For a moment, I thought I might drown anyway.

I was just about to give in when I saw him. "Help!" I yelled again. The warden looked over and then began to freak out, yelling out in a language I didn't understand. The water was pouring out of my cell now and into the surrounding ones.

The warden pulled the alarm and my cell flew open taking me with it and slamming me against the now slimy wall as the bars retracted. The warden hauled me out and dumped me unceremoniously on the gangway before I could get my breath back and so I lay there gasping as the warden pulled Zahi and some other guy from the two cells around mine that were now filling with water. He must've had his pay cut for dead prisoners or something. Otherwise I don't think he would've cared.

"Alexandria?" Zahi asked, his voice sounded like sandpaper, but it was his voice.

I flung my arms around him. "I'm so glad your safe," I whispered.

Zahi hugged me back. "I always knew you'd get us out again," he whispered back.

"We're not out yet, Zahi."

"We're a lot closer than we were," he said. "Where to now? Quick while all the guards are distracted."

I cast my eyes about the space. Metal walkways linked the cells together, but they were full of prison workers running to try and contain the problem. The alarm had released the bars on all of the cages, not just my own, and everywhere I looked other prisoners were trying to climb out of their cells only to be thrown back in by the workers.

That's when I felt the hole in the world. It was like a shimmer of light, but it was invisible to my eyes. It had to be a rift; a passage between realms.

"Do you feel it, Zahi?"

Zahi looked at me, confused, then suddenly he stiffened and nodded.

"On the count of three," I said. "One."

"Two."

"Three," we said together and then we took off. I had always been a sprinter and now I ran as fast as I possibly could towards the spot of air that felt lighter than the others. Even so, Zahi was ahead of me when the guards spotted us.

"Stop them!"

The cry went out but it was too late, Zahi was already through the rift.

I felt a hand grab my shoulder but I ducked out from underneath it and I too was through the rift between worlds.

We came out on a hillside in the evening glow of the setting sun.

"We're free," Zahi breathed beside me.

"We're free," I repeated, smiling up into the sky. I took a deep breath of fresh air and relaxed into the grassy hill, enjoying the warmth of the setting sun. I didn't know where we were, or how we'd find our way again. But we were safe, we were together, and we were alive; and that's all that mattered.

η

Chapter 8

Looking out over the grassy hills, an enormous weight lifted from my shoulders. After the interminable darkness the sunlight was both a relief and a curse and I had to spend several minutes with my hands over my eyes before I adjusted to the sudden bright light.

We might have been in Ireland, or perhaps Wales. My European geography was sketchy at best but I remember those two places being filled with rolling green hills.

"Have you ever seen anything like it?" Zahi asked, coming to stand beside me.

I shook my head and fell back against the hill to watch the clouds. The ground was damp but I didn't care. I was still sopping wet from flooding my cell anyway. It was strange to think of that place now; it was like a bad dream.

"How are we ever going to find Dacia?" I asked propping myself up on my elbows. We didn't have anything but the clothes on our back. We had to get back to our horses. We had to pick our lives back up.

Zahi bit his lip. "Walk, I guess. We have to figure out where we are."

"The middle of nowhere," I groaned laying back down.

"Hey it's not the end of the world."

"No, we've already been there."

Zahi laughed. "You can be such a pessimist sometimes you know that?" He asked, laying down beside me.

"It's hard to think of anything being difficult when the world seems so perfect in this moment." The clouds rushed overhead like they do before a storm. Perhaps it was going to rain. We never did find out.

"Are you two going to lie around there all day or were you going to do something about your situation?"

Zahi turned to me and smiled. "We got out of one situation today already, Dacia. How many more do we need to face?"

I started laughing then and I didn't stop until my lungs were burning for want of oxygen. It had been too long since I'd felt the euphoria of joy.

How Dacia knew where we were she still hasn't told me. She *did* tell me that she'd come back shortly after we'd disappeared and pieced together what had happened from the eyewitness accounts. My family knew I was safe, they hadn't worried.

"You two look like death itself," Dacia commented as she gave us our horses. I smiled with tears in my eyes as I greeted Ace. I had missed her and her calming presence.

"You're a good girl," I whispered, mounting up. All of my muscles screamed in protest, it had been a long time since I had used them and the escape had taken its toll.

"Neither of you have asked me where you are yet," Dacia said. "I'm ashamed. I thought I had taught you something." There was humor in her voice; I had no idea what she found funny about the situation, and I answered exasperated.

"All right then. Where are we Dacia? Where did we come out, how did you know we were here?"

"Welcome, my students, to the fourth realm, the first of the upper worlds."

The fourth realm. I looked around myself curiously, trying to sense the differences. Perhaps it was the surreal beauty that made this realm feel special. I didn't see anything else. But all the realms had a surreal beauty to them. Even the one I came from. Frustrated I closed my eyes. What made this realm different?

At once the exhaustion I had been ignoring crashed in on me like water in a pool when you've jumped in, clinging and pressing, suffocating with its denseness. I wanted nothing more than to fall asleep; to fall flat and let myself wander into my dreams.

"Woah." I heard Zahi dimly as he gasped and my eyes flew back open.

"It's dark," I blinked again. It was still dark. "Where did the sun go?" I asked, confused.

"It set, Alexandria."

"How could it have set in the blink of an eye?"

"Alexandria, look," Zahi pointed down the hill.

At the bottom was a town, a booming city really, with lights that shone like beacons, washing out the starlight above.

"That's not possible," I whispered.

"An awful lot is possible if you try. This is the fourth realm, a realm where time and space are as fluid as thought. There is a lot we can experience and learn here."

"But Dacia, we never finished learning our last lesson," Zahi protested.

"Did you not? You learned to sense the world, and you made a mistake and paid the price. If you didn't learn anything from all that I am sorely disappointed in you."

"Some things you can't change. At least not in the obvious way," I stated, staring down the hill to the town. Dacia was right. She had warned us against getting involved; said we weren't ready. We hadn't been.

"Dacia?" I asked. "How does traveling between the worlds work? Why did we end up in the lowest realm before but this realm now? Why don't we ever appear in the same places?"

I dismounted from Ace while Dacia contemplated my question; staring at me as if she could pierce my soul with her gaze. Ace nudged my back and I turned to rub her neck; after admonishing her verbally for pushing me. It was a bad habit that I shouldn't encourage.

"I will tell you about traveling," Dacia finally said. "You have a right to know the basics. It might help prevent anything like what you experienced from happening again. But no lessons today. It's late and you two have been through more than most experience in a lifetime; unless there is a war. In a way I guess this is a war," Dacia trailed off.

For the first time since getting out of prison, I wondered where she had gone when she'd left us. It had left a mark in her manner; her wisdom and assurance seemed shaken, like she didn't know what to teach us anymore. Or at least in what order to teach it.

"Dacia?" Zahi asked.

"Hmm, oh yes. No more questions tonight. Plenty of time for that tomorrow. You two have a lot more to learn and quickly. I am going to need your help soon; much sooner than I had anticipated. Let's get you two a proper meal, yes?"

A proper meal. That sounded like heaven to my ears; Zahi and I were skin and bones after our time in the cells. It would take weeks before we looked normal again, and for a long time we were both haunted by nightmares of that place. Every night I dreamt of that dark hole, of being alone and frightened.

I had always feared capture. Well, now I had been captured and I had survived. That has fueled me on ever since. No matter what happens I know that that square dirt hole in the ground will always be worse.

Time marched on, and we healed.

{[I][I][I][I]}

We didn't see much of the fourth realm for the first six months we were there, but we learned about it every day. We learned about the fluidity of time and space and how they coalesced into this world we found ourselves in.

There didn't seem to be any correlation between our thoughts and the time of day though occasionally they coincided. It was like the world had a mind of its own. Or perhaps it listened to someone, somewhere who had created this realm.

Dacia emphasized that it wasn't our job to learn to control the time and space of this realm. It was in our nature—as humans, our ego's seek control—but it wasn't in our destiny. The fourth realm required that our minds be as fluid as the realm itself. It was the epitome of "go with the flow."

"Dacia you never did tell us about traveling. How do we control it?"

"Again with control, Alexandria. There is no commanding nature."

"But there are ways to determine the world you go to, are there not?"

"She's right Dacia, you always know where you're going," Zahi cut in.

"There are mindsets you can be in to encourage certain rifts to open," Dacia began with a resigned sigh.

"Alexandria, what were you feeling the first time you went through a rift?"

"Fear." I replied immediately. "I was terrified of what was happening, and I wanted to escape."

"But you didn't escape. You went to a place where fear and terror reigned." She paused for a moment as I digested that. "And what about the second time, when you escaped."

"Relief, I guess. I was relieved there was a way out. And I was ecstatic. I was absolutely ecstatic that it had worked, that I was leaving that place."

"And so you came here, to the first of the upper realms, a realm more peaceful than your own and infinitely more peaceful the lowest realm. You would be safe here."

"So you go where you heart takes you. Or... no, you go where your thoughts and emotions take you?"

Dacia smiled. "It is a little bit of both, I believe. But sometimes, you just end up where you need to be. The Universe is vast, and mysterious. Even the wisest cannot completely comprehend everything that goes on and why."

I nodded. Before this "school" I found it incomprehensible why people would invest themselves in tasks they could never truly finish. Why would you ever try to get a grasp something so unknown as The Universe? It was an impossible task, but I had known people who thrived on that side of the spectrum; future scientists, researchers, archeologists. All of them loved to delve deep into the recesses of ancient texts and jumbled theorems seeking to understand the world or to find a way to make it better.

That wasn't me. It hadn't been, at least. But I was starting to understand deep inside what drove these people to comb through the miscellaneous ends of the known universe; to expand it in our minds with the idea that someday, somehow, we might find where it ends.

Our lessons were not particularly strenuous over these first six months in the fourth realm, though they were constant. We learned more about the chakras, from Dacia's point of view, and not just the stuff we'd been able to track down in libraries and the internet. But mostly, we spent our days in the barn. It wasn't large, just a four stall block of a building settled in among the grasses as if it had sprung from them. But it was safe and secure.

The dirt path leading from our back door to the cement flooring of the barn was entrenched with its surroundings just as much as the barn itself, though the rain had done its best to wash it away, leaving the dirt with furrows a plenty. One of the first things we had done upon arriving was even out the path to get rid of the tripping hazard the furrows caused. However, the first rainstorm erased all of our careful work and keeping the path even became a regular chore.

When the path was even, it was covered in hoof prints and boot prints that left neat little indents on the soft surface. Zahi would go out and take pictures at dusk; catching the last light of the evening as it shone across the top of the barn, lighting the horses in an ethereal orange glow and highlighting the shadows of the prints on the path.

His pictures were downright gorgeous and he made a pretty penny selling the prints on market day in the city.

When we first arrived, the entire property was in shambles, but together Zahi and I brought both it and ourselves into respectable condition. We started with the immediate and easy tasks. We cleared the pastures of harmful weeds and rocks, made sure the fence was sturdy.

Gradually the two of us got our strength back and we were able to work for longer and do more strenuous activity. We repainted the property, fixed the leaky roof on the barn, and rehung the doors that had warped from poor hinges and wet weather. There was a lot of wood damage in the house and in the barn and Zahi and I spent a good three weeks replacing it all.

Dacia worked in the house most days, though she was glad to instruct us on how to use our tools. I don't think I'd ever even touched a hammer before leaving home. Now I could probably build a house single handedly (granted it would take forever, but I could do it).

Though a lot of what we were learning was philosophical, I found I was much better prepared to handle the world now. I still missed my family, but I wouldn't have traded this experience for anything. It calmed my soul and in my heart I knew that this was what I wanted to do for the rest of my life.

{[]][]][[]]}

Riding was a blessing in disguise. There are those in the world who will try to tell you it is not a real sport; they are misguided. Like several unknown sports, it uses almost all the muscles in your body. Plus, it has the added difficulty of involving another living creature who has a mind and nature of its own.

Zahi and I regained much of our strength by working with the horses on a daily basis. Dacia borrowed a fourth horse from a girl in the village who broke her leg, giving Zahi and I each two horses to work with. I spent hours in the barn, slowly brushing the horses until they gleamed, taking the time to comb their manes and tails. It had been a long time since I'd tried to comb Ace's tail and it took me most of a day.

I combed it in the field where she could eat since I knew it would take me forever. I think the availability of food kept her annoyance level of me detangling way down.

We had a radio in the barn and Zahi would often catch me singing to the horses as I worked.

Overall, we stayed outside as much as we could, staring up at the bright blue sky that had for so long been out of reach.

Perhaps we would always be haunted by the prison. But I didn't think so. We knew that it was haunting us. We would be able to heal. Already the nightmares had lessened. We no longer spent nights huddled under the bright lights of the living room, playing board games because we were afraid to fall asleep and let the darkness of night take us off into the unknown of dreams.

The first nightmare had been the worst. I had woken screaming as I relived the escape. Except in the nightmare, I hadn't escaped, I had just kept drowning, with no one to help me and nowhere to go, trapped in the suffocating wet. It entered my lungs and filled them up until I awoke, terrified.

Zahi had nightmares too, different nightmares. Sometimes we dreamt of the same things; the walls closing in on us, escaping only to find an inescapable labyrinth...

But it had gotten better. We were sleeping again, we were filling out physically, our strength was returning, and our spirits were building.

We asked Dacia questions with fervor instead of dread; we spent rainy days with blindfolds on, practicing seeing the world without our eyes. The rain would pound down making it harder to hear each other's footsteps, the hum of the appliances, and the swish of clothing. But we adapted; we learned.

I was increasingly becoming more grateful for every moment I breathed, I had a new appreciation of just how fragile life could be, and I appreciated that I was still around to enjoy it. In this realm of fluidity, I learned to let time go. It didn't matter how long something took; chores took as long as they took and then we'd go onto the next thing. It didn't matter what time it was: if we were hungry, we ate; if we were tired, we slept.

We were fairly isolated, there on that farm. I spent a lot of time working with Zahi or learning with Dacia and Zahi, but I also spent a lot of time alone, reveling in the solitude that had previously seemed so lonely. Because I wasn't alone here, not really. I had people that I knew cared about me. I knew creatures that adored me and counted on me. Dacia managed to find us books and I would spend hours perched on a pile of hay, watching the horses and losing myself in the stories.

I began to connect more with a lot of the characters. I knew deep fear; I knew adventure and helping and selflessness. Well, not really that last one, but I could imagine it a lot better. It was back then that I began to plan out this book in my mind—this tale of my lessons and adventures in Dacia's mysterious school. Other people needed to know this stuff and what better way to share it than through the world's only clear source of magic?

{[|][|][|][|]}

"Reality is amorphous; if it has a form, it is one we force it into to fit our conceptions. There is no getting around this rule. If we perceive reality as spirit and infinite, then we will never find the end. But if we define reality as some tangible form and not spirit, we will find that end. Once we reach the end, however, we have no purpose in creation. That is the way of thought and mind."

"And the basis of philosophy," I grumbled. I had never cared for philosophers. They made your head hurt with their continuing questions that shook your perceptions of reality. But that doesn't mean that they're wrong. Rather the philosophers probably know the universe better than anyone other than the theoretical physicists. But I wasn't either of those. I hadn't even enjoyed those subjects.

Dacia laughed. "I think you will agree, Alexandria, that we go far beyond what philosophers dare to believe."

"How many realms are there, Dacia?" I asked. I was so used to the time fluidity at this point I almost forgot we weren't on the Earth, in the Milky Way; at least not the Earth and Milky Way I had grown up with.

"How many do you think there are, Alexandria?"

I shrugged.

"Oh, come on, Alexandria. Take a stab at it. How many realms to do you think there are?"

"Well, there are at least two lower realms and our realm—the middle world—and the one we're in, so more than four." I answered.

"And everything has to be balanced so that means there must be at least one more upper realms but an even number," Zahi added, "so six?"

Dacia smiled. "There are five," she said. "But you two were very close."

"How can there be five if there is supposed to be balance?" Zahi asked.

I was with him—it was all quite confusing.

"There are two lower realms, a middle realm, and two upper realms. With the five realms theorem we have, as usual, created a model where we are at the center. Some people however believe in a sixth realm that very few have traveled to. Most think it's a myth, but I believe it's there. I believe our realm is a lower realm and there is a third upper realm beyond our reach.

"We travel to realms that we can believe in—that we can imagine. I think the sixth realm is just so pure, so utopian, that we can't comprehend it," she paused then added, "And so we have trouble getting there."

Dacia was quiet for a while.

"Do you want to go there?" I asked.

Dacia smiled, but it was a sad smile. "It is every traveler's dream to see the great utopian realm," she whispered.

A pure utopia. Surely there was no such thing. But perhaps Dacia was on to something. Just because we can't believe something, doesn't mean it's not true. It just doesn't fit in our conception of reality and is therefore dismissed.

θ

Chapter 9

When Dacia was assured that Zahi and I had recovered, she began taking us into town. Though we had spent the last six months learning about the first four realms, it still didn't prepare us for seeing a fourth realm city in person. Compost and recycling were on every block; there were solar powered street lamps, zero-emission cars, and gleaming storefronts, even in the suburbs. Most of all, the people were happy.

That was perhaps the biggest difference: everyone was smiling. There was no rushing about, no mass of cellphone-talking zombies, just casual commuters strolling down the blocks, admiring their beautiful city.

"What's wrong with this?" I asked.

"What do you mean?" Zahi shot back, furrowing his eyebrows.

"Well, if this isn't the pure utopia, there must be something wrong with it, right?"

"The fourth realm is a brighter reflection of the middle realm we come from. In the middle realm this city is still a booming metropolis, highly advanced. Here you see the city as the people want it to be. If we traveled to a poor country, and then on to a poor village, you would see people going about their business just the same, but they would have sufficient food and water that they wouldn't have in the middle realm," Dacia explained.

"So this realm is more like a fusion of wishes, desires and freewill?"

"It is a reflection, or projection, of the positive character traits, many of which are linked to dreams. So in a way, yes, in a way, no."

That was clarifying. Not. But I could see what Dacia was getting at. In the second realm, there were positive thoughts and emotions but they were vague, undefined, and indistinguishable from each other. Here it was the opposite, the negative thoughts and emotions were the indistinguishable mush. If there was a political upheaval there would be a collective feeling of negativity, but no one would know what it was, only what caused the negativity, and they would correct the problem.

"I wouldn't mind living here," I muttered as we passed a children's park. Their joyful screams rent the air as they dashed about. I could hardly remember being that young and carefree.

"Why is that, Alexandria?" Dacia asked. Evidently she had heard me.

"It just seems so much simpler here."

"How so?" Zahi questioned, swatting at a bug.

I shrugged not quite able to articulate myself. "I don't know. I guess being able to easily identify where the negativity or dark shadow in your life is coming from appeals to me."

Dacia nodded appreciatively. "There are merits to such a design. But don't you think it might help to know why it is negative and dark?"

"Perhaps. I suppose if you knew the cause you could try and repair it rather than cut it out of your life."

"What about you, Zahi?" Dacia asked, "Would you prefer being able to always identify the negativity? Or being able to understand the cause when you do manage to find it exists?"

Zahi bit his lip, and I could see the answer in his eyes before he said it. "The second one, I believe."

"Why?" It blurted out of my mouth before I could stop it. I wanted to stop it; it was rude. If he wanted to tell us, he would have. Now he would feel obligated to tell us; he was like that.

"If you lost someone," Zahi began. "That would leave a negative emotion, wouldn't it? Sadness. But that negative emotion isn't a bad thing necessarily. It's a side-effect of love. You miss someone because you loved them and now they're gone. If you didn't know that what you were feeling was sadness, then you might just... forget. You might forget about the person you lost because that would get rid of the negativity. But that's not right. You shouldn't forget them... You just shouldn't."

He lapsed into silence and I looked down at the pavement in shame. We hadn't brought the horses today, and the city was no place for them. So we were walking with the rest of the people along the concrete sidewalks that could have been poured yesterday.

I wanted to tell Zahi that it wasn't like that. That people didn't overcome their negative emotions by forgetting about what they believed to be the cause. But I had no way to prove that. My words would be empty and fall on deaf ears. Zahi knew neither of us could assure him he was wrong, so he wasn't listening.

Dacia put a hand on his shoulder and we both got the message, "It was all right."

It was sometimes easy to forget that we hadn't always wandered the worlds together. We all had a past that we never talked about. Zahi had lost his parents, I knew that much and I knew a lot about his life before that, but I realized I knew little to nothing of the past of either of my companions. I didn't even know Dacia's full name.

The thought disconcerted me for a while. But then I thought, why does a person's past even matter? The past is the past, the present is now. It is only the here and now that really matters. In the fourth realm, more than any of the others, that made sense to me. When time is fluid you can't spend all your time focusing on what had happened or what will happen. You just focus on what's happening now and the world projects what the mind perceives.

{[][][][]}

After a few more weeks we moved on. Dacia said there was change afoot and we were off, riding across the country and attracting all sorts of strange glances.

"Why do we always ride places?" I asked Dacia as we rode out of the city. The girl with the broken leg had healed and taken her horse back, and the lease we had on the house was up. All the loose ends, neatly tied up with a bow.

"It is common to view the horse as a method of traveling. They are a bridge between the worlds, between places. All the lands on the Earth you know were found using ship and horse."

That didn't really answer my question. Perhaps it was a traditional thing, or perhaps it was symbolic. Symbols are important. Ideas of magic, religion, even science, revolve around symbols and symbolism. The cross, the elements, an ankh, a pentagram. There is a way things are done in the world; the President of the United States is required to give a State of the Union address yearly; however the senate has to invite him to give it. Such an exercise is pointless in reality, if something is required why must an invitation be issued? But no one changes the rules because it's tradition; a symbol of the cooperation between the branches of government and the separation of power.

The horses were symbols of movement and discovery and so we use them to travel, although there are many other modern ways to get from point A to point B. But that's just the thing, with modern travel there is only point A to point B. With the horses, or just walking, you could go anywhere on land. Steep mountain? Too steep to drive or use any other metal moving contraption? You can always climb.

The horses were excited to be going somewhere new. They were like small children being shown a place they'd never seen before. Wide-eyed and eager they took it all in. It doesn't matter that they've seen grass their entire lives, or that the sky is always blue. This was *new* grass, it could be different; this was a new part of the sky, maybe it was home to new creatures. It takes longer than we're there for the novelty to wear off and so they are faced with novelty after novelty, each one more unique then the next in their minds.

A bird took off from the bushes and Ace jumped backwards.

"It's all right, girl," I told her, carefully scanning the ground for more surprising wildlife. I didn't blame her for being spooked. It had scared me as well.

Horses are funny about what they find spooky, but then again, I guess we are too. We're scared of heights, scared of spiders; they're scared of loud noises, strange objects. Perhaps we're not as different from animals as we'd like to believe. Genetically we share more than half our DNA with most living creatures on the planet we call home. We forget, sometimes, we're animals too.

Whenever there is subjugation—a dictator enslaving his people, discrimination against minorities—an idea is propagated that the subjects are animal-like, that they are less then human. But humans *are* animals. In science class kids dissect cats and pig hearts because they have similar organs. Biologists test theories on mice because they apparently react similarly to we do.

So why is being degraded to an "animal" so negative. That is what we are.

{[][][][]}

Dacia led us to the seaside, the ocean stretching out to the horizon where blue met blue. The white sand was blinding under the bright sun and I found myself wishing I had sunglasses. I wasn't entirely sure there *were* sunglasses in this realm...

All of the houses were clustered past the beach in little rows stretching out from the pier which was lined with the entirety of the town.

"Why here, Dacia?" I asked.

"Change is coming and I want you to be around to see it."

"What will seeing change accomplish?" Zahi asked.

"If you know what it looks like when its carried out successfully you'll be better equipped to start it now, won't you?"

She had a point there.

But as to what the change was, she wouldn't tell us. Instead, we stabled the horses where we were staying and she sent us out into the town. "Find out."

Instructions, but not particularly specific ones.

The town smelled of fish and the salt of the sea spray but no one particularly seemed to care. The pier went on for miles out into the ocean so boats could dock in the deep waters, and fishermen could get good catches by just casting over the edge. Judging by the number of kids running about with kites and frisbees and swimming gear, school must have been out too.

Zahi and I took refuge at a clear spot in between two venders on the pier rail and looked out over the crashing waves.

"I always found the ocean to be peaceful," I said breathing deep.

"It's nice to see something so eternal and persistent," he murmured.

I nodded. Water is a powerful force with the ability to turn even the mightiest mountain to dust if given enough time. It's awe-inspiring.

"Do you think it's significant that Dacia brought us to watch some mystical change happen in a town on the ocean? After all, the ocean hardly ever changes."

Zahi shrugged, "Perhaps," he sighed. "Everything Dacia does has a meaning and a purpose. I just wish we knew what was going to happen, so we could be... prepared."

I understood what he was saying. The last time we'd been involved in a change we'd been arrested in the lowest realm and sentenced to life in the dark holes they called prison. We'd been reborn from the darkness like phoenixes rising from the ashes. We had a new outlook on life—a new appreciation for the light.

I didn't want to do that again.

My thoughts must have been in line with the realm because suddenly we were watching the sunset on the horizon.

"And so the day sinks into night and the darkness swallows the light winning the chase across the skies," I whispered.

Zahi chuckled. "That was quite poetic."

"Thanks."

"If it's getting dark should we go back?" he wondered.

"We've been here for under ten minutes! There are things to be discovered still. We have time. There is always time in this realm."

I grabbed his hand and together we darted back out into the crowd, dodging fishmongers and mothers gathering their children, shoppers taking their purchases home and elders out for a nighttime stroll, until we came up on a news stand nestled cleanly between a vegetable stand and the grocers.

"Voilà! News. Enlightenment at its finest."

"You know in our realm I'm pretty sure nobody actually reads the paper anymore," Zahi pointed out as he unfolded the section I had handed him.

"Yes well, you take what you can get."

Turns out all we needed was the front page headline: "Governor of 30 years Passes Away."

Not sure why Dacia couldn't have just told us the leader of this place had passed.

Zahi and I scoured the newspaper for details; apparently the same family had been elected to the role of Governor for the past three generations and for the first time in almost a hundred years there was no heir to run for the position.

We spent the next few days interviewing people about the old governor, pretending we had to write a paper for school. It was apparently a plausible story, or people just really wanted to talk about him.

From what we gathered the people were long since fed up with the more monarchial than democratic government, and change was a welcome event.

"The first man was decent leader, the best governor we'd ever seen," one old lady told me. She had been a child when Derrick Emery I had been elected. "When he announced he was going to retire due to his failing health, the people were in an uproar! It was such a fuss. I remember people mourning him as if he'd died! Can you imagine?"

"No ma'am I can't," I replied honestly.

"Well, at any rate when his son announced he would run you can imagine the people's delight. We hoped he was his father in miniature, I guess: a youth reincarnation."

"Was he?"

"Hmm?"

"Was he his father in miniature?" I asked, raising my voice slightly and speaking very clearly. I think her hearing aid battery needed replacing.

"Well he wasn't quite what we had imagined him to be. There were rumors he consorted with the women in the office," she stage-whispered as if it was the worst thing in the world. It was bad, but I had heard of politicians doing worse. The government hadn't exactly been well thought of at home. "But he ran the government fair enough I suppose."

"So why did you elect *his* son?" I asked. "You elected Derrick Emery II because you thought he'd be like his father, why'd you elect Derrick Emery III?" Also how had this family managed to have one child and have it be a boy for three subsequent generations? It was rather bizarre.

"Well, we knew him! Or we thought we did." The old woman continued. "He was a babe when his grandfather was elected and so we saw him grow up. At each public event he was a little bit bigger, a little bit older. And all his teachers swore he was the sweetest boy they ever had taught. Why when he ran for office he had his own fan club! Though that could have been his good looks and charm."

I smiled in spite of myself. I could just imagine this governor being chased by a grouping of screaming girls. It was a funny image.

"So he was like a rock star governor?" I asked.

"Oh yes," the woman said. "He was quite the fellow. But he couldn't govern to save his life," she sighed. "Every decision he made was a bad one it seemed. The economy's in the dump they say, our taxes have never been higher."

It was vaguely ironic this woman thought the old governor to be a handsome devil that every girl wanted. He had never married, and had no issue (well no issue that anyone knew about). There was no Derrick Emery IV to run for office. After over ninety years of being ruled by the same family (apparently the system was so weighted once you were in office it was impossible to be voted out despite the elections every six years) the people were ready for change.

The people had a choice. They could choose what kind of society they wanted to become. And, more importantly, after the experience they had, the people were willing to establish an entire new system of governing. It really was change in the making. A monumental decision that would affect the direction of the district for decades to come, and we were there to watch it happen.

Change wasn't brought about by fighting or by forcing the old family out. It was brought about by patience and dedication. The monarchial "democracy" was left to die in a corner, alone and forgotten, and a new age began.

Chapter 10

"What do you think they'll do?" I asked Zahi as I licked the ice cream cone I'd bought from the parlor across the street. Like all the days since we'd been there, it was warm and sunny so the two of us were in shorts and t-shirts and lathered in sun screen.

"Hard to say. They need to find a way to save the economy soon though."

"Have you asked Dacia about it?"

"Yes, but it does no good. I think she knows exactly how they'll resolve their lack of leader but she refuses to tell me."

"She probably doesn't want to be wrong," I sighed. "It would ruin her wise all-knowing image."

Zahi rolled his eyes at me. He did that when he disagreed; an annoying habit of his.

As the day progressed we noticed people kept congregating near the government buildings, standing patiently in groups as they discussed something. By noon, when we took a break to go to lunch in the nearby diner we could see nearly half the town congregated in the square outside.

"What's going on do you think?" I asked.

Zahi shrugged as he ate, swallowing before answering. "We should infiltrate the crowd and see if we can find out. It looks important."

My skin crawled as I remembered the last time we'd gotten caught up in a crowd. "Do you think it's safe?"

Zahi bit his lip and sighed. "Do you have a better idea?" he asked sounding equally unwilling to be in the crushing mass of people.

"No. Let's go before we lose our nerve."

Turns out the people were talking about the town. About what needed to be done and as people volunteered to do things, they would detach themselves from the crowd.

"Do you think they'll keep doing this?" Zahi asked as we watched the last of the crowd meander off some time later.

I shrugged. "Who can say? I guess we'll just keep watching."

We walked to the square shortly after waking up and I found myself watching the white fluffy clouds roll across the sky as we waited to see if any people would show up. I'd always found moving clouds fascinating. How fast must the wind be blowing all the way up there in the sky to make the clouds move so fast?

I was pretty sure it meant a storm was coming, though, with such iconic events taking place, perhaps we were in for a metaphorical storm just as surely as a physical one.

Time seemed to stand still that day. Perhaps it did, perhaps it was just our perception.

But at some point, people began congregating in the square again, and dividing up responsibilities. Zahi and I tried but could not determine who was leading such a mission. It was just...happening.

"This can't possibly be a sustainable form of government!" I argued after we'd witnessed ten separate congregations of this kind. Zahi told me I was being cynical again; so I set a new goal for myself. I would believe the best of everyone instead of the worst. It was still difficult to believe that such a model of government could work.

When I told Dacia this she smiled at me and said, "Once you believe in yourself, the only thing left to do is to believe in everybody else. If the people want this to work, it will. They are moving towards a oneness of mind. There is no need for hierarchy because everyone is on the same page."

"It's still difficult to believe that could really happen."

Dacia smiled, a little sadly. "That is because in the middle realm where we come from such a practice is still but a dream. We yearn for it to work yet the shades, particularly greed, seek to thwart every attempt."

"Is there any hope we may achieve such a oneness in the middle realm?"

"There is always hope, Alexandria. The oneness exists in this realm because there is hope in the middle realm. The idea is projected up through the dimensions and embodied where it is possible."

"How can we help the middle realm get to such a point where the oneness is possible?"

"Gently. We can help plant the idea in people's minds, make it a goal to be reached. We can preach about believing in themselves and in the world."

"People believe in themselves already," I countered.

"Do they, Alexandria? All the time, with all their heart?"

I bit my lip and thought about that.

I hadn't always believed in myself, it was true, but recently I had felt grounded as I never had before. I no longer had to tell myself to meditate, to stop and look and just be. It was all becoming intrinsic and the peace that that brought to me was immense and powerful. It filled my heart and soul with quiet not unlike the silent rays of the sun. I felt at one with the world and it gave me faith in myself.

Perhaps that is what Dacia meant. Perhaps if everybody in the middle realm felt like that, we could achieve a oneness of mind rendering hierarchy obsolete.

{[]][[]][[]][[]]}

We left the next day. Well, we left after the next time we woke up. The people who resided in this world had managed to create an entire civilization that functioned just fine in the fluid time stream, but I had yet to master how they managed. One day the sun rose then it skipped right over to the other horizon and sank again but the town didn't function any differently.

I genuinely hoped that we would stay long enough in the fourth realm to discover their secret but I had a feeling we were bound for something further then another fourth-realm city.

"Where are we going?" I asked futilely. Asking didn't do any good. Because it wasn't always the destination that was important. Sometimes all we cared about was the journey. Now was one of those times. For months we simply wandered the wilderness, following a river. When we were tired we put up tents and we camped for the night. When we awoke, we rode on.

Dacia said all the realms had the same geography as the one we grew up in and the same climate patterns as well. That may have been true but I doubt the population disbursement was the same. We traveled without ever seeing another city or town. It was like the rural areas had been wiped clean of civilization, only the cities existed.

It was brilliant. All the people were clustered in cities and suburban areas that faded out into wilderness where the wildlife grew and roamed freely. When this occurred to me I asked Dacia about the more threatening creatures we might come across, like large cats or wolves. Would we be in danger of being stampeded or eaten?

"There are places where there are dangerous predators, to be sure," Dacia began. "But this strip we've been traveling in was fire damaged many, many years ago. The small critters are just beginning to move back in. We've got a while before the predators follow."

That made me feel better. I had no desire to be eaten by a lion in my sleep. I figured this was the kind of place where lions might hunt. There was lots of tall grass, it was fairly hot and could have been Africa. But I was no geographical expert; we could have been in western North America for all I knew. In a way, seeing wildlife would have been helpful; then I would have known where we were to a more accurate degree. I knew we were going west and then we turned north, but beyond that I was completely lost.

Eventually we managed to tire at the same time the sun set. Zahi and I smiled to each other as we dismounted, big, wide smiles of childish joy. It was dark, we were camping. That meant *campfire*.

Together we cleared a spot of grass and leaves until just bare dirt remained—it was easier to contain the fire that way—and then we gathered wood. We had managed to pick a particularly beautiful spot that night; the river running along one side and a thick forest along the other with our campsite nestled in between.

Zahi and I passed the time while our food was heating over the flames freaking each other out. Taking turns, we theorized what animals could be hiding in the woods, waiting to jump out and eat innocent travelers as they slept on the creature's doorstep.

The guesses got more and more ludicrous and we were soon cracking up as well as looking over our shoulders for mythical predators.

"A spotted panther with a coat the color of the night sky and spots to look like stars that flies from the tree tops and crushes its prey by lying on it," Zahi whispered theatrically. "The victims swear in the afterworld that they were smothered by the sky itself."

"A race of men whose flesh has turned to bark and their teeth to razors. They creep towards camp and the forest itself seems to be moving to devour the wandering prey."

Zahi laughed. "Carnivorous trees," he cried. "Oh that's a good story. I need life insurance; my brother was eaten by the apple tree."

I laughed too. It wasn't particularly funny in concept, but the cartoon image it conjured in your head was hilarious in its bizarreness.

"The two of you could write horror stories for children," Dacia commented as she sat down with her dinner. Dacia had long ago bought a small camp oven for heating our food and so it was a rare occasion that we got to make genuine campfire food.

"I'm not sure many children like horror stories," Zahi said, taking a large bite.

"You'd be surprised," I responded. "My little brother loves them."

"Your brother is a weirdo."

"Yes, but that was unrelated to the horror stories."

I continued eating my dinner and looked up at the sky. The stars were brilliantly bright, dotting the inky dark like glitter. There were so many more of them in this realm—well, we could see so many more of them in this realm. It was stunning what a difference the lack of light pollution made. Like most things I hadn't ever really noticed it until it was gone, but now that it was I realized just how much we were missing by lighting up the sky with our artificial bulbs.

"If we put out the fire, would we be able to see the Milky Way?" I asked.

"Probably not with the full moon out. The light of the Milky Way is so faint you really need absolute darkness to see it."

One day I'd liked to see the Milky Way. The Northern Lights too. A lot of people think of natural wonders of the world as the Grand Canyon or the Great Barrier Reef. The Aurora is on that list too. I think it would be amazing to see the colored particles floating and dancing up in the sky. I think the Milky Way should be on that list too, but perhaps since it's in space it doesn't count as "of the world."

If we ever travelled into space, would we come up with new lists? The seven wonders of the solar system? The seven wonders of the galaxy?

Perhaps one day there will be trips out into space to see natural phenomena. We could go to a nebula and see baby stars, or visit far off interacting galaxies that form unique shapes. I heard there was one that looked like a rose.

"Do you think we'll ever travel through space?" I asked, laying down to watch for shooting stars.

Zahi lay down too and sighed. "You never know. We do always seem to be exploring. Always off to find new frontiers. Maybe we'll make it out there, someday."

"Why do you two want to explore space?" Dacia asked mildly.

"It's possibility isn't it?" I replied. "A vast unknown just waiting to be explored, discoveries waiting at every turn."

"Is that not what we're doing? Hopping between realms seeing how they differ?" Dacia pointed out.

"But it's not the same," Zahi said. "We're not the first to visit the five balanced realms."

"You likely wouldn't be the first to visit the far reaches of space either," Dacia said.

"But there's the possibility isn't there?" I threw my arms up and gestured to the skies. "There's infinity up there supposedly. Always something new, always a new horizon. Surely we could manage to discover something new and exciting."

Dacia looked down at the two of us, "Yes. There is always a possibility," she finally said. "The possibilities in life are endless and timeless," she whispered.

"But not always practical," Zahi murmured.

I ignored him and turned my attention back to the stars. Everyone always says, "shoot for the stars." They represent the epitome of excellence. They are what we strive for, what we wish on, they find their way into religion, science, art. Great big balls of gas millions of lightyears away. A star is one of the primary sources of life on earth aside from water.

Space is cold. And dark. And silent. But stars are hope and potential. Whenever I feel lost or alone, which happens much more infrequently since my travels with Dacia and Zahi, I look up at the stars. I look at the stars and I imagine whoever I'm missing doing the same thing, and suddenly I don't feel alone anymore. We may not all look at the same stars, but when we look at them I bet we feel the same things and that is incredibly unifying.

So much of our time is spent on trying to differentiate ourselves from the masses. "We are unique!" we shout. "We're not like everybody else. We are who we are and we like it that way."

All the stars are different too. Each one has unique chemical properties, a unique gravitational pull based on its mass and density. Every star has an age, has an orbit, has a life expectancy. Each one different.

And yet, they all have each of those things. They may be different values, but the concepts still exist.

More importantly, by the time our eyes detect the light emanating from a star all these billions of miles away they all look they exact same: little pinpricks of light up in the sky blanketed by the navy night sky and indistinguishable from each other.

Star upon star upon star, all right there in front of us and I don't think I could name a single one. I might know one, maybe two constellations and a handful of planets that look like stars, but that's it.

We may feel unique and individualized. However, from a distance, over time, over space, a billion years from now a billion miles away, we are all just the same. We are just like the stars.

"You've gone quiet, Alexandria," Dacia remarked.

I shrugged. "I was just thinking."

"About?"

"The stars. How much we are like them."

Zahi raised his eyebrows. "I'd never thought much about that. But they have always made me smile. Perhaps that is why."

Just as I was about to close my eyes to sleep, I looked up into the sky one last time and I saw it, a single shooting star slicing through the sky.

"I wish," I whispered, with a hint of a smile. There was nothing I could think to wish for. I was at peace in my heart and my mind and that was enough.

I dropped into my dreams where I was as infinite as the sky above my sleeping form. My soul a watchword for the world I strove to help protect as I soured above it, unlimited by physical form as I would be when I woke up once more.

In dreams anything is possible. With the right mindset, the same is true in life.

ια

Chapter 11

The next day we passed through a rift. One moment it was bright and sunny and warm and the next it was pouring rain. Dark ominous clouds rolled through the sky as water rushed down in torrents. Thunder cracked and lightning forked and the horses began to rear.

"Dismount!" Dacia yelled to be heard over the howling wind.

"Dacia we need to find cover!" I yelled back, quickly swinging to the ground between thunder claps. We must have been near the center of the storm; the thunder and lightning came together. I attached a lead to Ace's bridle so when the next clap came and she shied, I was able to turn her in a circle until she calmed down. I was glad she was a small-ish horse, it was easier to keep her from breaking away from me.

"Dacia, how far are we from civilization!" Zahi screamed as Fadia tried to bolt. Fadia was at least two hands taller than Ace and a lot more heavily built. I was impressed Zahi was managing to hang on to her.

"Half-a-mile, max!" Dacia replied, turning part way around. "This way!"

I didn't know how she was able to figure that out, I could barely tell where *she* was through all the rain let alone which direction we were going or should head in.

Looking back, it was a miracle we weren't struck by lightning. I guess we weren't the shortest path to ground; or we were just simply lucky.

When we found a local barn the man in charge just took us in, no questions asked, though he did grumble a lot at being disturbed during dinner. The barn was warm and dry but none of us were. As the man went back up to his house we began stripping the horses of the gear and tack. I hoped the place we were staying had a dryer; nothing was even remotely dry. I didn't think I would be dry again for years.

The thunder still cracked outside but it was fainter now and the horses were no longer trying to bolt with every clap. I'm not sure whether it was because they were inside now or because they'd gotten used to it.

"Why did we have to go through a rift at that precise moment?" I tried to ask through my chattering teeth. I wished I had a dry blanket to wrap around me but there was nothing dry we could use, not even to dry off the horses. We had to settle for using a sweat scraper to fling the excess water from their coats. Luckily it was warm enough in the barn we weren't particularly worried about them getting chilled.

"It was rather bad timing wasn't it?" Dacia responded. "But there is no checking before the leap. It's like a trust exercise between you and the universe."

"Well, I think the universe could have been a little kinder," Zahi muttered, rolling his eyes as he put Fadia up in her freshly bedded stall.

"It does seem to always put us in spitting distance of an open boarding facility," I said shrugging.

"Half a mile is not spitting distance," Zahi argued. "I bet we could have gone in any direction and found a town with a barn eventually."

"You two forget I've done this for a long time, I know which places will have spots and when. There are patterns to such things," Dacia said. She sighed and hobbled forward to the pile of wet gear. It suddenly struck me how old Dacia was. She was in great shape for her age and she was often spritely enough, but she was far from young and right now she looked it.

"Do you need help?" I asked, moving to help her anyway I could.

Dacia smiled at me appreciatively. "The weather is no fun with my old bones," she said. "The cold and damp seem to seep through the skin and make brittle what should be strong."

I nodded. Even I felt like that sometimes and I was still a teenager.

"So how far away is our place of residence," Zahi asked.

I laughed quietly. Only he would ask that in such a weird way. Though I totally understood, we never knew what kind of dwelling we would be in when we arrived in a new place. Dacia knew though. Dacia always knew.

"Just a couple blocks," Dacia said as she settled into a rustic chair in the barn isle.

"We should wait for the rain to let up a tad though."

Zahi and I agreed. It was still torrential outside and neither of us wished to be drowned more than we already were.

It was kind of nice, sitting in the barn aisle. Listening to the rain beat down on the tin roof and the horses chewing on their hay. The gentle rustling of the other horses and the clean smell of fresh rainwater as it bounced off the ground outside.

I breathed deeply and closed my eyes letting the sounds lull me to sleep.

"There's something about the rain that makes me feel so alive sometimes," Zahi whispered. Dacia had gotten up to look at the other horses in the barn and so we were alone for a bit.

"Rain is essential to life just as much as the sun," I answered. "Rain and sunlight working together to make the plants grow tall and strong."

"Do you remember the April rains we used to get?" Zahi asked. "When the heavens emptied onto the soil overnight and when we awoke it was to tweeting birds and dew soaked tulips."

I smiled. "Yeah," I whispered. "I remember. It was always so warm when you walked outside you could practically feel the water evaporating."

"Somedays it was like you evaporated with it."

"It was like you evaporated," I repeated. "You evaporated Zahi. For five years you disappeared without a trace. Where were you? Where did you evaporate to?" I kept my voice low and soft but my sleepiness was gone. Five years. For five years my best friend had been lost to me, off in the foster system or so I thought. "How long was it before Dacia found you?" I rephrased my question.

Zahi stared at his palms. "It was three, maybe four years. I was still so angry, Lex."

Lex. I had forgotten he had called me that. He was the only person that had ever gotten away with calling me anything other than my full name. And I had forgotten.

"I wanted so badly just to scream. Or explode. The pressure was welling up inside me like a spring being compressed."

"Because you couldn't come to terms with what happened?" I asked.

"Maybe. I felt like I had accepted it. But it sucked, Alexandria. It sucked and I wanted to know why. I wanted to do... something. Anything."

I remember just staring at him, not knowing what to say. I had rarely seen him so worked up and for once I didn't know how to stop it. I didn't know how to calm him back down. I couldn't say "it was all right" because it wasn't. Zahi had lost his parents. He'd been shipped off to live in a home for orphan boys because they couldn't track down a single relative he may or may not have had back in his native country. Finally, I just prompted him to move on.

"And that's how Dacia found you." I stated. It wasn't a question. If I was wrong, he would contradict me. But he only nodded.

"She came to our home after a tornado came through. She was there to help, but I guess she saw something in me. Something worth helping. She told the people who ran the home she represented an elite school and that I was a prime candidate."

"Did you believe that?"

Zahi shrugged and began tearing a piece of stray hay into pieces. "I wanted to believe it, I think. I wanted to be somewhere, anywhere else then there. I wanted to sleep in my own room and be able to have possessions that wouldn't get broken by the little kids or stolen by the bullies. The counselor that we saw said I was just a normal boy, an angry rebellious teenager with a broken past. Dacia said that's exactly why she wanted me to come to her school."

"What did you do when you found out there was no school?" I asked. "Did she tell you before she took you from the foster home?"

Zahi nodded. "She told me what she did for a living, wandering about, searching for answers. I wanted that. I wanted answers."

"Have you found them yet?"

Zahi looked up and met my eyes as if searching them for the very answers he sought.

"I'm getting closer," he whispered.

I nodded, "Me too."

{[|][|][|][|]}

In the morning I decided we were in the second realm. The colors were duller, the world seemed flatter, no one smiled, and everyone looked like they were in a permanent state of grievance. I hadn't seen much of the first realm so I suppose it could have been that one, but I was pretty sure it was the second realm; the air didn't fill me with fear and suspicion. The first realm left one with a permanent feeling of being watched, an unnerving tingling between the shoulder blades.

The air in the second realm was only mildly disconcerting, thick like when its really humid, though it was normally dry as parchment outside.

When I asked Dacia to confirm my suspicions she acknowledged we were indeed in the second realm but when I told her my reasoning she'd simply raised an eyebrow.

I really needed more data on the realms. Spending a couple months in one place wasn't a good way to form adequate ideas about the whole of that dimension.

Even now I don't really know that much about the realms. But I know how they make me feel, and I know that everybody perceives them a little differently based on experiences and beliefs.

The place we were staying was an apartment that reminded me more of a hotel suite; fully furnished in matching patterns with three bedrooms, a bathroom, and a common area with a mini-fridge, a microwave, a coffee pot, and a television. It didn't leave much in the way of cooking but the landlord said there was a fully functioning kitchen near the main office.

My favorite part was the small Zen garden on the patio. Water trickled down through various stones into a mock-riverbed. I picked up one of the stones and was surprised by how smooth it was. Was it a real river stone? I wondered. Worn smooth by the constant river flowing above it? Or was it a man-made mass produced rock—sanded smooth in mock-realism?

"This is a nice place," Zahi commented coming out to join me.

"It's pretty nice," I replied. "I think my favorite place was the condo in our middle world, though."

Zahi shrugged. "I've been to worse," he said decidedly.

I smiled and rolled my eyes. "There are always better things and worse things. We are in a state of eternal middle—never reaching the top and never quite falling to the bottom."

"The middle isn't so bad."

"The middle is 98% of the world."

"That's if the top 1% is the best and the bottom 1% is the worst. I think you'll find even in those two fractions there is still room to grow or fall," Zahi contended.

I pursed my lips and sighed loudly in exasperation. "Whatever," I said, only slightly sarcastically.

"Come on you two, we'll be late!" Dacia called.

"Where are we going?" I asked Zahi.

"Beats me. Off to save the world perhaps."

"Haha. Maybe we are. You never know."

We weren't going to save the world. Not just then. We were going to the local homeless shelter to help hand out food to the people seeking refuge there. It was very humbling to be honest. These people had nothing but themselves and because of their situations some of them didn't even want that—those few would give anything to be anyone else. That really got to me and I wanted to help them in more ways than just helping hand out their dinner.

Over the next couple of weeks, I kept coming back, sometimes with Zahi, sometimes with Zahi and Dacia, but always I came back.

I got to know the people personally, especially those who were the most depressed.

What I did was try to make it better. I tried to give them something to look forward too even if that just meant a nice conversation. I went around to schools and apartment buildings and set up drives, all to get these people the things they needed. If that meant some nice clothes to go to a job interview that's what I did my best to find. If it meant getting razors and shaving cream and hairbrushes, then that's what I asked people to donate.

I was stunned by the number of people that needed the shelters and even more stunned that those who weren't were rarely in position to help. I had known this was a lower realm, but I hadn't realized that meant economically disadvantaged.

When I asked Dacia about it though she told me that it was just this town. There were some places in this realm that were very wealthy and had little to no homeless or fiscally endangered peoples and some places that teemed with them—just like the middle realm I called home.

That made me feel a little bit better but I still couldn't help feeling the unfairness of it all. There should have been a way to distribute the wealth of a planet evenly across all its inhabitants. No one should go hungry or have to worry about keeping a roof over their head. But that's reality sometimes. And as Zahi had said: It sucked.

I wanted to find a way to make people happy, especially if I couldn't figure out how to help them. In a way, bringing joy *is* helping. Maybe not in the way people expect or want, but it does help. A lot of times, it's the first step.

My favorite success story of my time working with the shelter centers around a girl a little older than me. She'd been in college when her parents died. All of their assets had been used to pay for the debts they had accumulated in their life and she'd been left with nothing. No degree, no job, no home. The possessions she had been left with were long since gone—sold off to pay for the next meal—and she really felt how far she had fallen.

I became her friend, I encouraged her to keep coming to the shelter even though it embarrassed her so that she could find the help she needed. We were about the same size so I gave her some of my clothes, I helped her look for a job and prepped her for the interviews. Within a month or two we had found her something. It wasn't a good job, but it was there and it paid enough for meals and a couple changes of clothes.

We didn't stop looking though. Now that she had a job, more places were willing to consider her and before long she had transferred to a job keeping the front desk at a travel agency. It wasn't what she wanted to do for her life but it paid for the bills on a decent apartment.

She had a job, she had a home, and she appreciated it. She had hit a rough patch, but she clawed her way out again. She never forgot, though, and whenever she had time, she volunteered at the shelter same as I did.

A lot of the people there liked her better because she understood what they were going through. I ran into her once, a fair time after that, and she told me that she was happy she'd lost everything.

I found that a little bizarre so I enquired after it and she said, "Falling down gave me a new perspective on life. It wasn't easy, but it's a part of who I am and I will never forget that. No one who's ever been in a similar position will. It also taught me that sometimes you can't get out of the hole by yourself. Sometimes you need someone else to help push you out."

That conversation really sticks in my mind and whenever I'm feeling like I've been pushed to the bottom of the pile I remember it and I think, "I can make it out of this. I can get through this."

I highly suggest that everyone find a quote they find particularly inspiring. Something your favorite celebrity or author said or maybe something a parent said. Something that when you look at it, it inspires you to face the world. Write it down and put it somewhere you'll remember. Maybe on your wall or in your favorite book. And whenever you feel lost, or down, or just need a little something to get you out of bed in the morning, look at the quote.

It serves as a little pick-me-up. A reminder that everything will work out in the end. That might take two decades, it might take two days. The trick is to just keep hanging in there and always try your best.

Chapter 11

ιβ

Chapter 12

Sometimes bad things happen and there's nothing we can do about it. Trains derail, nations go to war, hurricanes and tornadoes and tsunamis destroy cities. People turn to their deities, to science, or even their local news station to explain why these things happen.

They just do.

After all this time I firmly believe that everything happens for a reason, but don't ask me to tell you what that reason is—I don't know. When we first came to the second realm from the fourth everything felt wrong; and I don't think that was entirely the reintroduction of a linear time frame. It hadn't been so bad going from the first to the fourth even though the jump was bigger because we had gone from low-high. It was a whole lot harder to go from high to low that quickly.

We don't always notice when things get better, but we *always* notice when things get worse. Perhaps that's one of the reasons we can feel so lost and unsatisfied. We need to learn to notice when things get better.

It's not particularly hard, but it requires being aware and paying attention to everything. Not everybody has been taught to do that.

It was Zahi that first came up with the idea to test our hypothesis.

We pretended it was a school project again and we got a bunch of volunteers to come participate. One at a time they went into a closed room and one of us sat in the room with them while the other played with the lights.

When I sat in the room, I found I could always detect the changes, but I was also expecting them. The volunteer sat in the middle of the empty room and we stared at each other and then slowly, very slowly, Zahi began brightening the light as far as it would go. Very few people took notice. If they did the only reaction was to look at the lights in confusion.

Once the lights were bright though, Zahi began to dim them. Every single volunteer noticed the dimming lights before they had gotten back to their original brightness. Sometimes they'd just look around them, sometimes they asked me if there was something wrong with the lights. Occasionally the person would just blink rapidly and look confused. And by the time the lights got below their original level almost everyone asked, "Why is it getting darker?"

The surveys we asked them to take confirmed our suspicions.

It looked something like this:

During your session which of the following things happened? Check as many as apply:

       □ The lights dimmed
       □ the lights brightened
       □ the light didn't change

Overwhelmingly most volunteers checked "the lights dimmed" as the sole occurrence. There were those who noticed them brighten, and those that didn't think anything had happened, but overall they were the minority.

This may not be absolute proof. Statistically its probably insignificant because of the limited resources for the testing. But Zahi and I decided it confirmed our thesis well enough.

Dacia simply watched all these goings-on with silent amusement. She said she was "impressed at our tenacity to find answers to the questions we asked". I think that was a compliment.

At any rate, perhaps this logic is why we didn't notice the amalgamation sooner.

{[|][|][|][|]}

When we moved on from that village I was a little sad to see it go, but we were ready to move on. It was strange how easily I had adapted to the life of a wanderer. We found a place, we made friends, settled in, did some good, and then we moved on and didn't look back.

"What's the longest you've ever stayed in one place, Dacia?" I asked.

She had to think a long time about that. "Six years," she finally answered. "Since I started traveling the longest I ever stayed anywhere was six years."

"That's an awful long time," I said. It surprised me, six years was a really long time. Not necessarily to stay in one place because people sometimes spend their entire lives living in one place, but think about it. In six years you go from a ten-year old just starting to gain some independence to a sixteen-year old. In America you're off to drive, in some countries you can drink; you've gone through most of puberty. Six years is the majority of a decade. In six years you can go from a high-schooler to a college grad, single to married with kids.

"Why so long?" Zahi asked. I rolled my eyes. It was a tactless question and I was pretty sure we both knew the answer. The curiosity had gotten the best of him though. He was like a cat.

Dacia was silent and for a while I didn't think she would answer the question, but just as I'd lost interest, she told us a very simple explanation that gave me more questions that it answered. "There was something worth staying for. Something I did stay for, though everything told me I should move on. I should have moved on."

I was burning with curiosity but from the tone of Dacia's voice Zahi and I both knew the subject was closed. I tensed with frustration but I knew it was useless to do so. I took a couple deep breaths and I let it go. It's a trick I learned traveling with Dacia. You may think it's so hard to let something go but really its quite easy, you just have to tell your brain "it doesn't matter." With practice and repetition, it might even believe you.

{[][][][][]}

The next village was more like a tribe. We rode for a week or two and then Dacia gave in and we took a cross-continental train. Once in the proper country we still had to travel on horseback for several days, but it was better than the months it would have taken us to get there otherwise.

The tribal members were more than happy to share with us, especially since we were fairly self-sufficient; we had our own tents and could find food on our own.

They found us quite interesting at first. We were nomads wandering the lands and they wanted to know all about what we had seen. The language barrier was a struggle, but Dacia knew the local dialect, which helped.

However, Zahi and I were forced to pantomime to the best of our ability. Needless to say Dacia did the storytelling. Though I did get better at charades.

There weren't too many problems with the wildlife, though some large cat was seen prowling the tents one night sending everyone into a panic. Zahi, Dacia, and I stayed with the children the elders and many of the woman and some of the men while the volunteers went out to dispose of the problem.

We heard the shouts and the snarling but we never saw the beast. Apparently it was bad luck to wear the skin or eat the meat of a carnivore and so the hunters buried it as deep and as far away as they could from camp.

It made me wonder how many other times something similar had happened. How many other carcasses were buried out there? Were their ancestors buried by their prey? Or were there two separate graveyards?

I didn't ask Dacia. I didn't really want to know. Then I'd have nightmares about bones in the ground. I'd probably have them anyway.

Chapter 12

I wasn't entirely sure why we were there. Why this village? Why now? It was interesting though, to see them and to see them in the second realm where positive emotions were undistinguishable.

Looking back, it happened to the children first. Well, one child. Just the one and I didn't even notice at the time. I had a little of the language down, but I didn't need to know it to understand what he said. I asked him how his day was and he said, "It was good. I am happy now."

That was it. Just one sentence that foretold everything and I missed it. For a while I pretended it the language barrier that had caused me to miss the importance of his words. But no, he'd said happy in English.

Then again, perhaps it was because he said it in English that I paid no attention to his words. Maybe I assumed it was something I had said and he was just copying me. Little children have a tendency to do that.

But like I said, I missed it and it was another month or two before we started noticing things were off.

{[][][][][]}

It was a tribal holiday and the sun was shining as bright as it ever did in this dim realm. There was dance and song and smiles all around. If it hadn't been a monthly holiday I'm not sure we would have noticed the difference in the behavior. As it was we'd participated in the holiday two times previously and so when the leader changed the words, we noticed. Zahi and I had no idea what it meant, but we noticed and we went to find Dacia on the other side of the gathering.

Based on the frown she was wearing I knew she'd noticed too.

"Dacia the words are different," I murmured even though no one could understand me.

"That's not what concerns me," Dacia murmured back. But that's all she would say until the holiday was over. It wasn't polite to be talking during the rituals.

It wasn't until the sun had set and the festivities had turned to the adults discussing stuff around the fire that Dacia told us what the words had meant and the news was disquieting.

"They are not words that belong in this realm. I only recognized them because this dialect is similar to the tribe that lives in this spot in our middle realm."

"What words were they," Zahi pressed.

"Faithfulness, loyalty. He said, 'Let us enjoy what peace and happiness have brought to us.' among other things of a similar nature."

"But this world can't distinguish the positive emotions. It's all one thing to them," I said.

Dacia nodded. "They have a single word for that 'epano'. It translates roughly as 'up'. It's the only word I have ever heard them use in any positive emotional context."

"Dacia, what's going on?" I asked. I didn't remember the little boy saying, "happy." It was only much, much later that I remembered that's where it all began.

"I don't know, Alexandria. But I aim to find out. Will you two be all right on your own for a bit?"

"What, here?" Zahi's eyebrows shot into his hair.

"No, not here. You don't understand the language. We'll find a place."

"Why leave us at all, Dacia? We could help." I said.

"I'll think about it," Dacia said. That was the best we could do for now. The next day we set off again though we didn't leave the area. There were several other tribes within a three-day radius and so we made the rounds to each tribe. Sometimes they let us stay, other times Dacia was just able to ask a question before they shooed us off.

That was fine with us though, it was a very important question.

"Are you happy today?"

"Won't the language barrier be an issue?" I had asked her.

Dacia had shaken her head. "I think I know which dialect to use for each tribe. They are similar to the tribes in the next realm, I will just use that word."

"What if that doesn't work?" Zahi asked.

Dacia shrugged. "We'll think of something else."

Normally that something else meant convincing them to let us stay so Dacia could listen for new words in their vocabulary.

We found it wasn't happening in every tribe. The further from the first tribe we ventured the less likely we were to find new words. Whatever was going on seem to be localized.

For now.

"What does this mean, Dacia?" I asked. We had visited all the tribes by this point and were making our way to the nearest city.

"I'm not sure yet, Alexandria. I need more data."

"But you're not going to leave us again, are you?" Zahi asked. I understood his concern, the last time hadn't gone so well for us in the end, though that was entirely our fault.

"Yes, I will Zahi. But you won't be idle. I'll leave you in the city and I want you to stick around until you can determine if the positive leak is happening there too."

"What happens then?" I asked.

"You'll take the train to the next city on the map."

"So that's it? We just travel around the continent and listen for the words that shouldn't exist."

"Essentially yes. We need to discover where this is happening before we can go about determining why. I'll travel across the realms. Maybe I can figure out where its emanating from."

"How long should we stay in one place?" Zahi asked.

"Until you hear the positive leak."

Positive leak. That's what we called at the beginning. When we thought it was confined to that.

"What if we never hear it?" I asked.

"Then you won't be going anywhere," Dacia said firmly. "There won't be a need to if it's confined to this area."

"Where will we stay?" Zahi asked.

"Here," Dacia handed him a card not unlike a credit card but it wasn't any brand I'd seen before.

"Stay in hotels, mainly. Shift around the city if you don't hear anything after a week or so. This card should work anywhere in this realm."

"What about the horses?" I asked.

"There's a nice boarding place in the next city. They'll be safe there and I have an automatic payment system with the owner. He charges the account until we show up again."

"What if we never come back?" Zahi asked. I shot him a look.

"You shouldn't say stuff like that Zahi," I reprimanded him, rubbing Ace on the neck. I couldn't imagine my life without her.

Dacia smiled. "When the account runs out, which would take approximately ten years with his prices, he is to sell the horses to good families."

"What happens if you spend that time in the fourth realm and lose track of the time?" I worried.

"I never leave my horse in a different realm than I am in for precisely that reason."

The plan was quickly forming and soon we were in the city.

Dacia found us our first hotel, helped us stable the horses and then she left; gone like she had never existed.

"Part of me hopes we don't find anything," I admitted to Zahi as I stared out the hotel window. We were on the fifteenth floor and it was kind of weirding me out. I'd never been up so high before.

"That would be easier wouldn't it," he replied folding his clothes and putting them into one of the drawers.

"We forgot to ask him about laundry," I muttered.

Zahi laughed. "I'm sure we can find a laudromat somewhere," he said. "This city is ridiculously large.

I smiled. It wasn't that big, but it was definitely the largest one we'd visited since we'd begun to travel together.

"Do you want to go see the horses tomorrow? It's just one subway stop I think."

"It might rain tomorrow, but if it doesn't I think we should. Make sure they're settling in all right."

I nodded absently. It did look like rain.

"If we were to find something," I began. "Where do you think we'd hear it?"

I turned from the window and looked at Zahi critically. I felt we needed a plan of action.

"Well," he said. "I suppose we should go places where people are generally happy."

I thought about that. "So maybe a playground or something."

"If we want children yeah. I was thinking more about concerts though."

I nodded. "That could work too. Perhaps we could crash weddings or something. Birthday parties."

Zahi rolled his eyes. "I think we should stick to the legal end of the spectrum, Lex."

I laughed. "You're probably right. I wonder if there are any amusement parks nearby. People there tend to be happy, right? And happiness isn't the only positive emotion maybe we should search some other places too."

"The other positive emotions aren't as easy to identify I don't think. They all seem to include an element of happiness or contentment."

"I suppose," I sighed flopping down onto the bed. It was growing dark out now.

"So first thing tomorrow we make a list of places?" Zahi asked.

"Tomorrow," I agreed. Today had been a long day and if there was one thing the fourth realm had taught me it was this: there is always a tomorrow.

Chapter 13

The dawn broke early, flooding the room with sunlight as it peeked over the horizon. In retrospect it would have been smart to close the heavy drapes and not just the sheers.

The damage was done, however, and we were too awake to fall asleep again.

"So where did we say we were going to go first?" I asked, yawning.

"Park," Zahi replied copying my yawn. "And then the barn if it's not raining."

"I'm not sure anyone will be at park this early in the morning."

"We could just wander around the streets then I guess, get a feel for the city. None of our options are really occupied at seven a.m."

"I bet people'd be happy in a coffee shop."

"I could use some coffee," Zahi agreed.

And that is how we found ourselves in a little hole-in-the-wall coffee shop at eight in the morning in a strange city listening in on people's conversations.

I never was a big coffee drinker so I had a hot chocolate and a pastry; Zahi on the other hand was on his third cup of coffee. I wasn't sure he'd ever sleep again.

"Surely that much caffeine is bad for you."

"Hasn't killed me yet."

"You haven't been killed by a train yet either that doesn't mean you stand in its way."

Zahi threw a straw at me.

It had been a long time since I'd sat in a coffee shop. It was nice, relaxing. There's something about coffee shops, the dim lights, the smell of roasting beans, the comfy chairs. We returned there nearly every day before starting about our business, even when we'd moved to a different hotel across town, we came back because we loved the atmosphere so much.

So it's no surprise that that's where we first heard it.

Ironically we had slept in late so it was really more like lunchtime by the time we made it the coffee shop we adored.

A couple was sitting behind us on a lunch date. Just a normal scene. Then one of them said, "I love you," and that was that.

In this realm all positive emotions were expressed by saying, "I feel good" or some derivative of that expression. There was no word for love, there was no word for happy, they just didn't exist. And yet they did.

And so Zahi and I locked eyes. We knew what we had to do.

I said goodbye to Ace, Zahi said goodbye to Fadia and we packed our stuff. The train ride wasn't particularly long but it sure felt it as we sat there in silence. Our hearts were heavy with the idea of being separated from our horses and our minds bogged down with swirling thoughts. What was wrong with the realms?

There was nothing particularly remarkable about the next city, tall buildings made of brick, dirty sidewalks and graffiti. Scowling people going about their errands wishing they were anywhere else. It took us less time to find the positive leak this time but not by much.

In each subsequent city it happened sooner and sooner until all Zahi and I had to do was get off the train before we heard it: some child saying she was "so excited." So back on the train we got. We'd covered nearly an entire country by this time.

"What now?" I asked.

"Let's cross the border," Zahi responded. "How? We don't have proper papers or anything. There is no record of our existence in this world."

"We'll go back, get our horses and our camping gear and go over an unprotected part of the border."

"We can't sneak across borders!" I said, aghast he would even mention such a thing.

"Alexandria do you really think we haven't done that already?"

Now that I thought about it he was probably right. We'd covered so much ground in the various realms we probably *had* been illegally crossing borders.

"Well, there goes my perfect record," I muttered.

Zahi just shrugged.

So we took the train back to the first city we'd stayed in. As soon as we got off we could tell something had changed. We were hearing people expressing positive emotions everywhere we went. It got to the point I had to ask Zahi if we were still in the second realm or if we had somehow managed to get ourselves into the third realm.

Zahi shook his head. "This is definitely the second realm," he said. "Our horses are still here, and so is our coffee shop."

Zahi was right, but that only made it worse. Something was happening to the realms, they were... merging, it seemed.

"Zahi we need to talk to Dacia," I said.

He nodded. "I know, Lex but how are we ever going to find her?"

"I don't know."

"Then we'll stick to our plan. We have to see if its spread to other countries."

"We should check suburbs and towns too. We've only been visiting the cities."

It was great to see Ace again and to get back in the saddle. It had taken Zahi and I nearly five months of city hopping to determine that the entire country was affected and I had missed her terribly.

"You're my good girl," I whispered as she sniffed my hands. She seemed happy to see me—which was good because she wouldn't be leaving my side again for a while.

Zahi and I crossed the countryside on horseback, camping when it got dark, and setting out again at dawn. We traveled in as straight a line as we could, stopping in at civilization whenever we found it.

The positive leak had grown and it was traveling faster than we were. Often all we had to do was introduce ourselves and we could tell the area was affected.

They would say, "We're pleased to meet you."

Wrong answer. They should have said, "It's good to meet you." Or something.

And so we would move on. I was really getting worried now. It seemed as if the entire realm was being infected and Dacia was nowhere to be seen. I wanted desperately to go back to the middle realm, to see if it was all right, to see if my parents were all right.

Zahi calmed me down by pointing out we hadn't really seen anything alarming other than the introduction of language that didn't exist. And that wasn't harmful to a person's health or wellbeing.

He was right, I was being silly.

Nevertheless, I wished Dacia was there to explain it.

It was a dark and stormy day when we finally saw her again. Zahi and I were huddled in one of the tents praying the lightning wouldn't strike it. Outside the horses were uneasy in the temporary corral, but they seemed to be fine.

The thunder cracked right over head and I jumped as a figure suddenly appeared in the doorway to the tent. Apparently being centered with yourself and aligning your chakras and soul pieces etc. does not keep your adrenaline from reacting to jump scares.

So Zahi and I both jumped and screamed upon noticing the figure.

"Calm down, the two of you, I don't bite."

"Dacia!" I cried, relieved. "Where have you been?"

"Things are even worse than we thought," Dacia replied. "But we'll talk about that later. Tell me what you two have been up to."

And so we explained to her the routes we had taken and the words we had observed creeping into the language. We probably sounded terrified. We were terrified. Nothing Dacia had ever taught us had prepared us for this. I think what scared us more though was that Dacia looked worried. She looked worried and she looked old.

"So it's spreading through this realm," Dacia summarized when we had finished.

I nodded. "And it's getting faster and faster."

Dacia sighed.

"What were you doing, Dacia?" Zahi asked.

"I was visiting the other realms, trying to find anything incongruous."

"And did you find anything?" I asked though I was sure I already knew the answer.

"Yes," Dacia nodded.

The tea kettle whistle went off and Zahi got up to make us all a nice warm drink to ward off the fear and the cold.

"What's happening?" I whispered, sipping my cocoa.

"Near as I can tell the dimensions are collapsing.

"The dimensions are what?"

"Collapsing. Something has happened. Some sort of mixing that shouldn't happen. The balance of the Universe has been disrupted."

"How do we fix it?" Zahi and I asked, almost at the same time.

Dacia smiled sadly. "I knew you two were the right apprentices to pick," she sighed. "I tell you the entire world is falling apart at the seams and the first thing you want to do is fix it."

"*Can* we fix it?" I asked.

"Maybe, but we have to figure what happened first. Why is everything off balance?"

"Could it be the traveling?" Zahi asked.

Dacia shook her head. "That's been going on for centuries by people like us. That can't be the sole reason or surely we'd have noticed something before now."

It was solid logic but I couldn't help but think of a dam that breaks. The dam itself could have been damaged for ages, the reason it broke at just that moment was because the pressure behind the dam became too much for the weakened barrier.

What if traveling between the dimensional realms had the same effect as water pressure against a damaged wall?

"How are we going to figure out what went wrong?" We needed a plan. Plans were good. "And how did you know that the realms were collapsing?"

"I traveled throughout all five available dimensions. In the lower realms there seems to be a positive leak. The shades are becoming as hard to find as they are in our middle realm. In the upper realms the shades are taking over—countries are in turmoil, leaders are being ousted for the sake of anarchy." Dacia shook her head. "I haven't seen such a wreck since the world wars."

"Is there any good news?" I asked. My cocoa was gone and the storm was receding but we were all still on edge.

"They are still physically separate."

"What will happen if they merge, Dacia?" Zahi asked.

"Not even the wisest of us can tell."

And with that ominous thought she told us to go to bed.

It was only when I had lain down to sleep that I realized Dacia had never answered my question. How were we going to figure out what went wrong?

{[|][|][|][|]}

"Dacia," I asked the next morning while we ate breakfast on the dew-soaked grass before the horse corral, "Does this have anything to do with why you disappeared the first time?"

"No—" Dacia began and then abruptly cut off. She furrowed her eyebrows and then got up so quickly she spooked Fadia. "Finish up, we have to go."

"Go where?" Zahi asked before dumping the rest of his food into his mouth. It amazed me how much that boy could eat.

"We need to see a friend of mine. If we hurry, we can catch him before he jumps realms."

"What happens if he does jump realms?" I asked.

"Then it will be much harder to find him."

I probably could have figured that out on my own now that I thought about it.

And so in a flurry we collapsed the tent, rolled up the sleeping bags and mats, undid the horse corral and packed the poles into the saddle pack Dacia carried. It took us maybe thirty minutes max. I was rather impressed—it normally took closer to an hour.

We rode towards the sun as fast as we could without tiring out the horses. They seemed to sense our urgency and they flew across the ground with such ease I could almost imagine they were pegasi leaping through the air.

The dark of the night and the weight of our sore muscles forced us to stop till dawn, but as soon as the sun peaked over the distant horizon we were aiming for, off we went.

Before long we came to a small village nestled in the foothills of a mountain range.

"Is this it?" I asked. I had no desire to go galloping up the steep slopes.

"Yes," Dacia wheezed. "This is it. Look for the 'Lightwork Tavern.'"

It was a large restaurant, not far from the edge of town with a dark interior and sturdy wooden furniture. Dacia had us sit and order something to eat while she went up to talk to a man at the bar.

"Who do you suppose that is?" I asked Zahi as we stared from our table.

"He's got to be another traveler if Dacia's asking for his advice."

The two of us had to avert our gazes quickly as Dacia and the strange man looked over at us. The man was definitely younger than Dacia — his hair was not yet gray— but other than that I couldn't really tell much about him. It was too dark and they were too far away.

"Why do you think Dacia is asking his advice at all? Do you think that's who Dacia went to help when she left us in the third realm?"

"It's gotta be," Zahi replied. "I bet you were right. I bet the dimensional realms collapsing *does* have something to do with that."

Our food had come by the time Dacia and the man came to join us.

"Sandor this is Alexandria and Zahi. This is Sandor, he's agreed to help us out." Up close the man was slightly frightening. His hair stuck up straight and wild like he'd been recently electrocuted, his eyes seemed to point in different directions, and he obviously hadn't shaved or had a bath in quite a long time.

"Are you a traveller?" Zahi asked as soon Sandor sat down.

One of the corners of the man's mouth twitched up. "Yes, I am, lad," he replied with a thick Scottish accent. "And I take it the two o' ya are Dacia's apprentices."

We nodded. "She's been teaching us what she knows," I added.

"That's bound to take a while," Sandor said with a chuckle. "Dacia 'ere 'as been travellin' as long as anyone I know."

"Do you know what's going on?" I asked.

Sandor shook his head. "I'd noticed somethin' was off but it wasn't until Dacia told me that I realize how bad it 'ad gotten."

"How are you going to help us?" Zahi asked.

"You two are curious aren't ya. I'm gonna 'elp ya because I know where to start lookin'."

"Where is that?" Zahi and I asked almost simultaneously causing Sandor to laugh again.

He looked at Dacia for permission and then began to explain. "A while back, there was a traveller that went missin'. We looked for 'im and 'is apprentices everywhere but there was no sign o' the man, the two girls, or the little boy."

"That must have been a difficult search," I murmured.

"It was indeed. We contacted everyone we knew to 'elp look."

"That's why you left us, Dacia." Zahi stated.

Dacia nodded but didn't say anything, instead she just kept eating her salad.

"Do you think the missing travelers have something to do with the collapse?" I asked.

"It might just," Sandor replied with a wink. "I can take you to the village where 'e was last seen. After that you want to talk to Jacqueline. She's been trackin' the case."

Dacia nodded thoughtfully. "Do you happen to know how far she's gotten in deducing what happened to them?" she asked Sandor.

"Last I 'eard the evidence suggested goin' rogue."

"Going rogue?" I asked.

"It's an...archaic term," Dacia replied. "It refers to a traveller who has turned their back on helping and turned to hurting instead. But is she absolutely sure that's what happened?" She asked insistently turning to Sandor.

Sandor shook his shaggy head. "No, I don' believe so."

Dacia nodded, her blue eyes looking far off into the distance as if she could see through space and time itself. "We'll leave at dawn."

"Shouldn't we rest the horses more than that?" I asked. "We've pushed them pretty hard the last two days."

Dacia pursed her lips but she nodded. "Yes. We should. We'll give them an extra day and hire some pack horses to lessen the weight."

"I know jus' the man to see," Sandor said. "Don' you worry 'bout a thin'."

I did worry though, all that night and into the morning until Zahi told me to go meditate out on the balcony of the hotel we were staying at.

I managed to calm my heart and balance myself but I was on the edge of a knife in the sink. A little wobble either direction and I would drown.

This was turning out to be bigger than anything we'd ever seen before and I had a notion that this time Zahi and I weren't just going to be innocent bystanders. This time, we'd be the epicenter.

Chapter 14

The mountain pass was a narrow gorge barely the width of the horses that led through the towering rock that soared upwards so high it looked as if the top was touching the sun. Sandor assured me that no one had died in the pass for years. That did *not* increase my confidence in the idea of sliding between two mountains.

Nevertheless, the canyon was stunning. All the layers of rock were visible, stacked up on top of each other and compressed into ribbons of color. They served as a reminder that what's inside is often more beautiful than what's on the outside.

I was reminded of how silent the wilderness of the second realm was, and how dark. The canyon brightened briefly around midday, when the sun was at its peak and could shine down into the gorge. But time moved on and the sun passed the opening, plunging us all into the gloomy twilight of the gorge once again. There were no creatures in the gap, no predators to spring down on us from on high or trap us within the narrow confines. For that, I was grateful, but it would have been nice to hear birdsong.

The linear fashion we were forced to travel in made conversation difficult and so we walked in silence, each of us lost in our own thoughts.

I'm not sure what the others were thinking about, but my thoughts were focused on the missing traveler and his three apprentices.

It was still strange to me to think that Dacia, Zahi and I were not the only people to hop across the realms, though I wasn't surprised. How many of us were there though? How many people knew the truth about the dimensions of the universe? Did we all originate from the third realm? Or were there travelers from all the realms?

I shook my head, forgetting I was thinking to myself. I couldn't imagine there being travelers from the bottom two realms; they were too consumed by the shades. I remember when I had been like that, I still get like that, on occasion. I haven't hit enlightenment yet, I'm not perfect, but I know how to overcome the shades. I know how to escape their captivating hold. In a lot of ways, the dark hole of prison in the first realm taught me that. Dacia had told us the basics, but it was the darkness that let me see the light.

"End in sight!" Sandor called from the front. I jerked my head up and strained to see past him, sure enough a little ways ahead the mountains stopped and the gorge widened out into a field.

Freedom. Well, that's how I thought of it. In the gorge we were confined to walk rigidly in a single line in a specific order and a specific pace; out in the open we were free to do whatever we wanted. Likely we wouldn't change our formation at all except maybe walk two by two instead of single file. But the options we had could span pages. We could gallop sideways for all the good it would do. Freedom is the ability to do whatever. Common sense is doing the right thing despite the freedom to do the wrong thing.

We broke through the mountain and were welcomed with the same twilight atmosphere we had just left. I turned around just in time to see the last rays of sun sink below the mountains above and then dusk reigned.

"Should we stop?" I asked. It would be dark soon after all.

Sandor shook his head. "The moon will be out strong tonight. We can make it to the village under its light."

I shrugged. He was the boss of this mission. We did pick up the pace though and trotted until the trees overhead blocked out too much of the light to continue safely. I'm not sure Sandor remembered to calculate them into his estimation of available light.

Nevertheless, we plowed on, picking our way carefully across the uneven forest floor. The leaves were still on the trees, there was no crunch of their remnants underfoot, the twigs were either too small to make much noise or they didn't exist because I couldn't hear the small snaps as the horses stepped on them. The silence was deafening.

It was like we were ghosts, flitting through the trees—nonexistent entities who left not a mark in their wake.

Every now and then the trees would thin and we would see the full moon shining bright. Its silvery sheen seemed to give it a halo as the invisible sun reflected off its gray rubble surface. Scientists say that it's home to craters and mountains but I can't see any of that from atop my horse. All I see is a giant disk in the sky with hints of shadows that suggest it's 3D.

I needed some sleep if I was starting to compare the moon to a flying saucer.

I shook my head and blinked several times trying to wake myself up. Riding is like driving, you should always be alert.

"Are we almost there?" Zahi asked with a yawn.

"Not quite," Dacia called back. Like that was helpful. It had been a long four days and really I just wanted to sleep.

But the road wore on and the darkness deepened and still we walked through the silent night.

The inky black was an abyss stretching on forever. The desire to see the bottom is so compelling, until you lose your balance and topple to your death. It was treacherous; ready to swallow its prey at a moment's notice and drag them down to their doom.

"Lex," Zahi said softly. The path had widened up and our horses walked in tandem for a bit while we talked.

"Yeah," I replied, rubbing my eyes to try and banish the sleep.

"Where do you think the travelers disappeared to?"

I shrugged. "Likely they're all dead somewhere," I whispered. I hated to think it but the odds were with it. "It makes my heart hurt," I added and it was true. I wanted so badly for this to have a happy ending but I could feel it slipping away with every breath. Nothing good would come of this.

Zahi nodded. "Yeah," he said and I knew he shared every one of my thoughts, even the unvoiced ones. "But how do you think it happened?"

"Anyway a death could happen, I suppose."

"Do you think they were on to the amalgamation? Or do you think they caused it?"

"Honestly, I think they caused it."

"How?"

I let out a harsh laugh that sounded more like a cough. "Zahi, I still can't tell you how we can hop realms. I can't even begin to imagine why they'd break."

Zahi chuckled.

"What's so funny?" I asked.

"You say 'break' so casually, like fixing it will be a matter of some glue and clamps."

I shrugged. "I don't know. I guess that's easier to think about then all of reality ceasing to exist as we know it."

"True."

A wolf howl broke through the still and silent night, making me jump.

"Dacia?" I asked, panic rising in my voice.

"Keep calm, they're still a ways off. Stick close and walk with purpose. We need to clear the trees."

"The tree line is still a long ways off, Dacia," Sandor said.

"We'll make it."

We bunched together and picked up the pace. It wasn't too difficult, the horses had heard the howling and knew what it meant. We had to hold them back to keep them from bolting headfirst into a tree.

It was too dark to take off. Dacia was right, we needed to clear the trees.

The howling was getting closer.

"They've picked up our scent, 'urry!" Sandor cried, letting his horse trot.

It was dangerous, but we had no choice. I let out the reins a smidge and Ace began trotting nervously, all the motion concentrated under herself.

"How much further?" Zahi called.

"More than I care for," Dacia replied.

I turned my head and thought I saw the faintest glimpse of yellow eyes.

"Dacia?" I asked, panic building again.

"We're almost there."

The wolves were visible now. They were still a ways back but they weren't being shy. We didn't have much time.

"We're there!" I looked forward at Sandor's cry and saw to my relief the trees disappearing. We let out our reins and the horses broke into a full gallop.

"They're in pursuit!" Zahi screamed to be heard over the howling and the pounding of hooves.

I looked under my arm and saw that he was right. "Come on girl," I whispered to Ace.

"Where's the town?" I asked.

"Half a mile!" Sandor called back. I was surprised he had heard me.

"Can we make it?"

"They're closing in!"

"It's a military base. If we make it to the town, we'll be safe."

And so we kept galloping. I tried not to look at the ground as it blurred by to keep my dinner in my stomach but it didn't help much. The queasiness kept growing and I wondered if it was a side effect of the adrenaline in my system or if I was really just that motion sick.

The wolves were barely five feet behind us and getting closer with every stride. The horses were tiring; after four days of traveling, they couldn't keep up the pace much longer.

I heard warning bells and suddenly a great light shone down on us.

Shots rang out and I heard a wolf yelp.

We were close.

"Ride!" A voice shouted through a megaphone.

I got closer to Ace's neck and prayed that the road was smooth as I asked her for one last burst of speed.

The gates of the compound closed with an ominous clang as soon as we were through and dimly I heard small thwacks as the wolves in front couldn't stop in time.

"I hope they're okay," I said.

"Lex they tried to kill us," Zahi panted.

"They were hungry!" I protested.

Sandor rolled his eyes.

"They can find someone else to munch on," he grumbled.

One of the guards from the gate ran down off the wall.

"What brings you here?" he asked not the least bit out of breath.

"We're looking for Jacqueline," Sandor said. "And a place to stay the night."

The man nodded. "I think something can be arranged given the circumstances. Security is strict but we don't want you eaten by wolves either."

I didn't care if we had to sleep on the cold concrete as long as I got to sleep. The adrenaline was fading and my will to stay standing was going with it.

Luckily it didn't take them long to find us a couple spare bunks in a barracks unit meant for guests. We put our horses in their makeshift corral in the middle of the grassy training green after promising to clean up after them and then I collapsed onto my bed, falling into a fitful sleep with nightmares full of snapping teeth and yellow eyes.

{[|][|][|][|]}

"I hear y'all are looking for me," a young-ish blond said sitting down to breakfast with us the next morning. She was older than I was certainly but she was practically a baby compared to Sandor and he was young when you thought of Dacia!

"You're Jacqueline?" I asked.

"In the flesh."

"Why are you in the military?" Zahi asked eyeing her uniform. "I thought you were a traveler."

"I can do both. I live in all worlds." Jacqueline defended. "I'm needed here for the moment."

"I thought you were investigating the missing travelers."

"That too. He disappeared near here. These soldiers were the last people to see him."

"Do they know anything?" Dacia asked.

Jacqueline shook her head. "If they do they're not telling. All I've gotten out of 'm is that he showed up, not unlike you four, spent a couple of days and left with his apprentices."

"And no sign of him anywhere? None of the neighboring cities or towns?"

Jacqueline shifted uncomfortably. "One of the girls was found," she finally said in a hush.

"Where?" Dacia asked.

"The river. Her body floated ashore."

I looked down at my food my appetite suddenly gone.

"You've searched the river for the others?" I verified.

Jacqueline nodded. "No sign of them. I don't think that's how they were traveling. The body showed signs of a struggle. It's likely the body was just disposed of in the river."

"Gotten an autopsy?" Sandor asked.

"Not yet. The specialist was off-base when we found her. He only recently returned."

"Jacqueline. Do you know what's happening?" Dacia asked.

Jacqueline furrowed her eyebrows in confusion. "I'm afraid I don't know what you're referring to," she answered honestly.

"You haven't noticed anything strange?" I asked.

"I assume you mean stranger than missing people."

We all nodded.

Jacqueline shrugged. "Not really, no. Why?"

"We have reason to believe the realms are collapsing," Dacia began, lowering her voice to avoid being overheard. "We've noticed palpable shifts in the distribution of the shades of emotion across the dimensional realms."

Jacqueline narrowed her eyes. "What do you mean?"

"We've heard people of this realm talk about being happy or excited or in love and Dacia said she saw anarchy in the fourth realm," I explained. "All five realms seem to be mirroring the balance in the third, middle, realm instead of their respective dimension."

"Now that you mention it I have heard some different vocabulary around here lately. I just assumed I'd been a little too free with it, or other travelers had, and influenced a localized positive effect."

"It's not localized. It's *everywhere*," Zahi said.

"And you think Jacobs has something to do with it," Jacqueline whispered.

"Jacobs?" I asked.

"The missin' traveler," Sandor filled Zahi and I in.

"Well, based on your reactions to Jacobs disappearance I imagine it's not often a traveler is veiled. If it's a rare occurrence, and the realm merge has never happened before, maybe they're linked," I reasoned.

"I suppose it's possible," Jacqueline allowed. "What do you suppose we do?"

"We need to track him down. Every trace, every atom."

"Dacia, I've been trying to do that for months and we've gotten nowhere."

"You found one of them. The autopsy might give us some clues."

"She 'as a point," Sandor said. "We're just that much closer."

"It's still not enough to go on," I pointed out. "I'm not sure we have much longer."

"Sandor how soon do you have to get back?" Dacia asked.

"I've got a day or two, why ya ask?"

"Can you go back the way of the river? Take a soldier with you, look for any clues on the riverbank, any more bodies."

"Thought you did that."

"We went up a dozen miles or so on either side but not much beyond that," Jacqueline clarified.

"This guy 'ad months on you and you only went up a dozen miles?"

"We were on a time constraint!" Jacqueline defended. "We didn't think the body could've made it further than that. Plus, my missing guy isn't particularly cared for by any of these doofs," she gestured around the mess hall, "they just think it's another story you hear in the news by the dozens."

Dacia nodded. "They wouldn't understand the importance. Take one of them anyway to report back anything you find. I'm sure someone can be spared."

"What are we going to do, Dacia?"

"First we'll wait for the autopsy report. Then we move out. Find out what Jacobs went off to find or do."

"Hope you have better luck than me," Jacqueline muttered.

"I know a few tricks," Dacia said mildly. "Though I admit it's a long shot. We rarely disclose our plans to anyone."

"Is this even possible?" I asked, a note of desperation finding its way into my voice.

Dacia nodded not really seeing what she was staring at. "It'll be difficult to be sure, but I refuse to believe it's impossible. There is always a trail."

Chapter 15

The autopsy came back the next day and with it a great feeling of dread seeped into the hearts of all involved.

"Blood loss," the pathologist said. "Not drowning."

"Where was she hurt?" Dacia asked.

"I don't think it was an accident," the pathologist replied. "The marks look very deliberately etched into her skin. Many of them were small enough that they would have clotted long before she lost enough blood. Someone was deliberately draining her."

"Why would anyone do that?" I asked in a hush.

"It's quite common with certain animal sacrifice rituals that the natives once used on this land. I haven't seen them used on a human before, though, and they say the last ritual sacrifice was decades ago when the settlers ran the natives off."

"Do you know where we could find someone from that tribe?"

The pathologist nodded. "They resettled about fifty miles north of here, follow the river bank."

"Is it possible that's where she came from?" Zahi asked.

The pathologist shook his head. "That river is one of the few in the world that flows backwards—south to north."

"Thank you for your help," Dacia said. "Alexandria go find Jacqueline. Zahi pack up the horses."

I ran off through the compound looking for the tell-tale blond hair. It was a large place, and I was panting heavily and nursing a wicked side-stitch by the time I found Jacqueline talking to a couple soldiers by a fence line. When she saw me she immediately excused herself and walked over to meet me.

"Whats up?"

"We're leaving. Dacia wants to see you."

"The autopsy came back?"

"Yeah, possible ritual sacrifice."

"What?!" Jacqueline squawked.

I nodded unable to get anymore words out.

"All right, let's go." Jacqueline ran off pulling me along behind her while I tried desperately not to fall on my face. I wasn't out of shape, per se, but it had been a long time since I'd done any sprinting, and riding used different muscles.

We stopped briefly while Jacqueline packed a bag and then we were off again to join Dacia and Zahi at the entrance gate.

"Ready?" Dacia asked Jacqueline.

She nodded. "Any ideas about the culprit?"

Dacia shook her head. "We'll find out though. I promise."

Loaded words. It's a dangerous thing to make promises. Just two words can make everything okay for the person who hears them. However, promises come with a pressure that can destroy the soul trying to keep them. A broken promise has a psychic energy wave akin to a tsunami as it overwhelms the soul with feelings of guilt and shame.

I mounted Ace and we rode through the gates, headed towards the forest.

"What about the wolves?" I asked.

"They moved off to hunt other prey," Jacqueline said. "They never stay long where there is nothing for them to eat."

I nodded but kept looking about me warily. I had no desire to run into any more dangerous wildlife. I think Ace felt the same way as she eyed everything with more caution then normal and her ears pricked at the slightest of noises.

"All right, let's pick up the pace. We can make it there before nightfall if we hurry."

And so yet again we took off. I hoped we would stay with the tribe a couple days. The horses would need their rest; they were still recovering from the previous adventures.

During a walking break I rode next to Zahi.

"Do you think they were all sacrificed?"

He shrugged. "I don't know. The whole thing is sketchy to me. Why would they sacrifice somebody and then dump them in the river? Aren't the bodies generally burned or buried, not just unceremoniously discarded?

"Honestly I know very little about human sacrifice, but you have a point. It does seem strange." I was silent for a bit until I couldn't help but ask, "Are we positive it was even a sacrifice? What if someone just really needed the blood?"

"For what? They're not vampires."

"I don't know, maybe blood transfusion or something, maybe a new health and beauty trick?"

"Those are both pretty sick reasons for killing a girl."

"The whole situation is sick," I grumbled. I was glad we'd never seen the body. It felt a tad dishonorable, but my imagination was horrid enough.

My thoughts were lost in the pounding of hooves and the beating of the sun as we picked up the pace again. I wished I had taken off my jacket before setting out, the warmth was going to baste me.

The trees disappeared into the distance and suddenly I was spitting sand out of my mouth as the horses kicked up the new footing.

"What's happening?" I asked curiously, slowing down to stop the sand from pelting my face. We seemed to have suddenly found ourselves in a desert.

"Very large beach," Jacqueline called back.

In confusion, I looked left at the snaking river we found ourselves following. "So the river runs into the ocean?" I asked. "Why can't we see the ocean from here if we've found the sand?"

"It's about nine miles of sand sloping uphill then a short drop off into the ocean. We can't see it from here because of that drop off."

"But why is the beach so large? Surely the trees would give way to beach grass or something this far back."

Jacqueline shrugged. "Superstitious people say the land is cursed. Nothing grows naturally in this stretch of land. We could probably introduce them though if we wanted."

I thought they should and I said so, but I don't know if they ever did. I'm not sure the base cares and I don't think the tribe has the resources.

It is a shame though because that spot has the potential to be very beautiful. It was beautiful already in its brown and yellow facade, the river cutting the otherwise smooth landscape in half. However, some plants would have really livened up the area and protected the sand dunes from erosion.

We made it to the tribal village just as the sun began to sink towards the horizon and to no one's surprise, Dacia could speak their language. However, it did surprise me to learn that the villagers spoke English as well.

"They have enough interaction with the base that they've picked up most of the language," Jacqueline said. "They're quite quick at learning. Sometimes I wish we could recruit some of them to the army instead of the handful of bozos that come with every shipment."

"I'm sure they have their share of intelligence diversities," I replied. I wasn't sure how Jacqueline was defining smart, but I was sure she wasn't doing it enough justice. Almost everyone has the ability to be intelligent with regard to at least one subject. I guess it's just the people who are gifted at nearly everything that get called smart, though.

Personally I think smart should be on par with talented. Society, however, doesn't appreciate that opinion because they view smart as logical, not creative. So someone who is not good at anything logic-based will not be considered smart. I don't think that's fair to them because they can do things traditionally smart people could never do.

But I didn't say any of this to Jacqueline.

Dacia didn't bring up the subject of the ritual sacrifices to the villagers for two days. I think she was afraid they would kick us out if they thought we were rude and intrusive. A valid worry, I think. If someone came to visit me and started prying into stuff my ancestors did, I'd be weirded out. Waiting made it seem more like curiosity.

First Dacia got them to trace the marks used in the ground, evidently the pathologist had shown the body to her because she said that those were the same markings.

The villagers were just as confused as we were as to what they would be doing on a human body but once they understood we didn't suspect them of the deed, they were more than willing to tell us about the rituals associated with those marks.

"They wanted the blood," the elder told us haltingly. He wasn't particularly good at speaking English and most of what he said was in his native tongue for Dacia to translate.

"What for?" I asked.

Dacia translated my question for the elder and then his response back to me.

"It was a story we used to tell," he said. "About the cruel gods who reigned before our time. Once a month they would come down from the heavens and take two people; the oldest and the youngest."

I bit my lip to keep from pointing out the logical fallacies in these gods' plan. I had a feeling they weren't particularly welcome thoughts. But seriously, if you kept taking people from a village faster than they could reproduce and then took those they reproduced the next time how did they expect their food supply to last? Unless they didn't eat them...

"What did they take the people for?" I asked when the elder paused.

"The stories did not say," the elder said. "But the village tried everything to protect themselves with no luck. Finally, a kind spirit from the river said 'to protect yourselves disguise your scent until you are naught but animal.'"

"The blood," I whispered, horrified. The elder nodded.

"You see the gods had no use for creatures who were not human. And so once a month the villagers would sacrifice one of their animals, paint its blood onto their skin, and wear blood soaked rags. The gods left them alone, not recognizing them as the human they wanted, and a new age of prosperity reigned."

"And the ritual?" Zahi asked. "Did you coat yourselves in blood for the same purpose?"

The elder shook his head frantically.

"We let out the lifeblood of the animals to honor our ancestors and appease the old gods so that they stay away for good. But the practice went out generations past."

Dacia nodded. "We understand," she said. "Has anyone else come asking about the ritual?"

The elder thought for a moment. "A long time ago," he said. "There was a boy. A young boy all on his own who said he was lost. We cared for him until his father came to claim him but in the meantime we taught him much about our culture; our history and our way of life."

"How long ago?" Dacia prodded.

"Maybe thirty by now," the elder shrugged. "We don't keep time quite the same as the cities."

Dacia nodded. "Thank you for telling us what you know," she said before leading us off. "Jacqueline what do you know of Jacobs?"

"Not much, not before he became a traveler at least."

"That's our next stop."

"What are you thinking, Dacia?" I asked. "You think that young boy the elder mentioned was Jacobs?"

"Could be, or maybe he's met him. Somehow someone knew about the ritual. Stories like that...they have power, there are roots of truth imbedded within mythology. We can't find Jacobs anywhere and we know someone was playing with rituals that hid humans from gods. There has *got* to be a connection."

Zahi and I nodded but Jacqueline just looked pensive.

"Dacia you're suggesting something akin to sorcery," she whispered. "That's not what we're a part of."

"Jacqueline I have long suspected there was something sinister surrounding Jacob's disappearance. If he has begun inflicting harm and spreading hate after swearing to spread love and uphold the peace and prosperity of the realms through positive energy, then that could have very well triggered the events we are seeing."

It was the first time we had heard Dacia's theory and it was a doozy. To suggest that Jacobs had killed his own apprentice? Preposterous. Horrible. But at the same time, it was the most likely explanation available.

"So what do we do?" I asked.

"Well we have to find proof don't we? Keep following the breadcrumbs, right Dacia?" Zahi responded.

Dacia nodded. "Keep following the breadcrumbs. We'll stick around, see if we can find out more about the boy and the man that came to pick him up. Jacqueline, how long till you have to get back?"

"I took my leave ma'am. My calling has changed; this is where I need to be."

"Understood. Well then, why don't you try and come at this from the other end."

"Jacobs's past?"

Dacia nodded, "If my instincts are correct, we'll meet up in the middle of his story. If not, well I'm sure we'll see each other again."

Jacqueline nodded and gave us a big smile. "It was nice to meet you two," she said turning to Zahi and I. Then she was off, riding into the distance until she vanished and I knew she'd gone through a rift.

"What realm is Jacobs from?" I asked.

"Third one I believe, which is why I think the man who came to get him was his teacher, not his father," Dacia said. "Though as Jacqueline said we don't know much about his past, about any of our pasts. We become new people when we choose to live the lives we do."

I nodded. I knew a lot of Zahi's past because we'd been friends before, but I knew nothing of Dacia's before I met her. And I really didn't have the desire to learn more; it was like Dacia said: the past didn't matter, it was the present we should be concerned with. Especially when the present seemed to be rapidly falling apart. This tribe was no different from any other area we'd seen in the second realm and defined positive emotions were creeping into every conversation.

"I forget sometimes that this is still the second realm," I told Zahi that night. "Once you get used to the flatness of everything, and with the positive leak, this might as well be our middle dimension."

"I know what you mean," he replied. "I've found that happens in all the realms, really. When you stay in them long enough they begin to feel like home."

"Have you been to all the realms?"

Zahi shook his head. "Just the first four."

Just then, Dacia and one of the older villagers came and sat with us to discuss the young boy. The woman had been his primary caretaker, serving as a foster mother of sorts.

"He was a sweet boy," she said, "but he did seem to have a curiosity for the more primal sides of life...and he had an 'eye for an eye' philosophy."

"Can you describe what he looked like?" Dacia asked.

The woman narrowed her eyes as she tried to recall his image. "He was blond, I remember that. So different from the rest of us, pale as the moon and incredibly thin and bony. We had some bony children too but Keelan was something else. It was like he was only bone and skin no matter what he ate."

That was a pleasant image. "Do you remember the man who came to get him?" I asked.

"He was quite tall, also thin. Graying dark hair and imposing. He was a rather threatening man."

"And he said he was the boy's father?"

"He said the boy was his charge and knew all about him. Keelan went with him gladly though he told me he would miss me." The woman looked off into the distance as if her memories were playing out right before her eyes.

"That was the last time we saw him," she said quietly.

"Do you know where they went?"

She shook her head and the conversation dissolved into tips on planting rotation crops.

"Keelan Jacobs?" I asked Zahi quietly.

"Would seem so, though we don't know that's his first name. Jacqueline would know."

"That she would. I wonder if she's found anything."

"If it was super important I'm sure she'd come back and tell us," Zahi reasoned.

"I bet Dacia knows too. Think she'll tell us later?"

"I'm sure. Though it does seem strange."

"Can apprentices be that young?" I asked.

"I guess they can. I mean, they're probably orphans or from a family of travelers."

"Travelers can have families?"

"Yeah, though it's not particularly common. Dacia said it pretty much only happens if two travelers fall in love."

"Can you ever be too old to be an apprentice?" I wondered.

"I know most apprentices are under twenty-five but I don't think that's a hard rule."

"That's probably when people are the most open to being apprentices," I murmured.

"Could be," Zahi agreed. "Could be they're more willing to change their opinions about the world. Grown-ups always seem to get stuck in their ways."

"I've met grown-ups willing to adapt," I said. "We all have things we refuse to change about our behavior."

"I guess," Zahi said but I could tell he didn't really believe me.

"Go to bed you two," Dacia called. "Early start tomorrow."

"I guess that was Jacobs," I said wryly, knowing we'd only leave the village if we had a lead to follow.

Zahi laughed. "Guess so, goodnight Lex."

"Night," I yawned. Tomorrow we were off to chase ghosts. What could go wrong?

Chapter 16

The fog clung to me like a damp rag, not heavy enough to be opaque, but damp. So damp, it was as if we were walking through a cloud. Which I guess we technically were...

"Where are we?" I asked, my voice sounding oddly hushed. We'd been traveling for days first heading northeast, then straight east, pushing the horses as safely as we could without exhausting them.

"Moors," Dacia grunted, pulling her scarf higher on her face.

"Aren't moors dangerous?" Zahi asked.

"Not inherently so long as you avoid know where the solid ground is, though they do seem to be a common setting for ghost stories," I replied casting a wary eye about. "Why are we in a moor?"

"Technically aren't quite yet," Dacia replied moments before I felt the shift in the air that signaled a rift.

The fog disappeared and the moors vastness took its place, stretching on around us until it met with the distant horizon.

I never get tired of hopping realms.

"The third realm?" I guessed. "To meet Jacqueline?"

"Right on both accounts, Alexandria."

"How are we going to find her?" Zahi asked.

"Oh we'll just find a village and ask," Dacia said. The wind picked up and I wished I was wearing something dry to cut its chill. I looked through my pack in vain, the fog had seeped through everything.

"How will that help?" I asked, trying to keep from shivering; Ace wouldn't appreciate it.

"Well, we know roughly where she started looking and what direction she said she was heading. She ought to be around here somewhere by now," she said, but I knew she was lying. Somehow Dacia just knew where people were. Maybe that's why she was so disturbed that no one could track down Jacobs; not even her.

"So what village are we looking for?" Zahi asked and I noticed his teeth chattered a bit. So I wasn't the only one who was cold. That was good to know, maybe we'd find shelter quicker or at least a place to dry our clothes.

Dacia thought for a moment and then pointed behind herself. "The nearest one is that way. They might have a laundromat where we can dry out our clothes and packs."

Dry. That sounded plenty good to me. I turned Ace about and we began to trot off to the south. It wasn't too long before the village in question came into view: a four-block main street, a couple of neighborhoods, apartment complexes, and agriculture farms.

Zahi got us a place at the inn, I found a place to keep the horses: where they stabled draft horses who worked on the agriculture farms, and Dacia went to get provisions and ask after Jacqueline. By the time I had settled the horses I was turning blue and my teeth were beginning to chatter hard enough that I worried I would bite my tongue by accident.

I practically ran back to the inn to get the blood flowing again and was rewarded with a hot room and dry clothes.

"Is D-dacia b-back yet?" I asked taking the stack of dry clothes from Zahi.

"Not yet but I thought I saw her at the bar downstairs about ten minutes ago, so she should be up soon."

I nodded. "You think she found Jacqueline?"

Zahi shrugged. "I didn't any sign of her but that doesn't mean anything."

I didn't think I would ever be dry again so I took a hot shower. I figured I would still be wet but at least I'd be warmer for it.

"Good grief are the two of you trying to catch on fire?" Dacia asked when she walked through the door to the room sometime later.

"We were cold!" I defended wrapping my blanket tighter around myself. Zahi and I were playing cards at the table by the fireplace and I was actually losing quite badly. "Did you hear anything about Jacqueline?"

"Innkeeper said she was here this morning but left for a day trip. Said she'd return in the evening."

"Do you think she will?"

Dacia nodded. "She's not one to deceive. She'll come back. In the meantime, you two should eat something. Order room service if you don't want to leave your boiling room."

"Where are you going?" Zahi asked as I attempted to make a play.

"Not far. The hall of records is open so I thought I might go take a peak."

"You need our help?" I asked putting down a random card and hoping it worked.

"Later. Zahi's busy whopping you."

No arguments there, that's why I wanted to get out of it.

Dacia winked and left again.

"You think she's avoiding us?" I asked idly in an attempt to distract Zahi from his cards.

"I think the 85-degree room threw her off. Hah!" Zahi threw down his last card with a triumphant call. "Let's play again."

I narrowed my eyes. "Fine, you win, but let's not. Is there any game I'm not horrible at?"

"Not that we have with us."

"Then why don't we get food instead."

Zahi shrugged and I grabbed the room service menu from a drawer while Zahi turned on the tv and found the local news channel. I had just decided that I was in the mood for breakfast foods when Zahi cursed.

"What's the matter?" I asked looking up at the tv screen. I too let out an expletive that my mother would not have approved of. "Turn the volume up."

"An earthquake of magnitude 9.2 devastated the west coast of America today obliterating several cities and causing damage throughout most of central California. The quake was reportedly felt in areas of Nevada and originated from a spot on the San Andreas fault near San Francisco," the reporter was saying as images of the damage was shown from a helicopter. "A quake this large hasn't been seen in America since the Alaskan quake in 1964 but already the fatalities are estimated to be in the thousands. Many countries are on alert for Tsunamis and most of Hawaii has already evacuated to high ground..."

Zahi hit mute and stared at me. I could see the fear in his eyes and knew it was mirrored in my own.

"Do you think it's related to what's going on?" I asked. "Or is it just a freak act of nature."

Zahi shook his head turning paler all the time. "I don't know," he whispered.

"We have to find Dacia."

"Yeah. We do."

We grabbed coats and ran out the door, barely remembering to grab our key before we were dashing out into the street and towards city hall, darting through pedestrians and traffic like our lives depended on it.

"What happened? You two look like you've seen a ghost," Dacia commented as we ran in. We'd gotten lost a few times on the way, but we still found her before she'd seen the news.

"Earthquake," I panted. "Big, big earthquake."

"Where?" Dacia slapped the papers she was looking through down on the desk and met my eyes with razor intensity.

"America. California. San Francisco," I wheezed. I really needed to run more often.

"How big?"

"9.2," Zahi answered.

"9.2?" Dacia clarified, her eyebrows shooting up.

We both nodded.

"Is it related?" I asked.

"Not to the cause, but perhaps to the effect," Dacia replied. "If the realms are attempting to merge together I have a feeling there will be natural disasters aplenty."

"So we don't have much time left?"

"Less and less," a grim voice came from the doorway.

"Jacqueline! We didn't expect you until nightfall," Dacia said with a smile.

"Got back early and saw these two dashing about the street," she gestured to Zahi and I.

"Did you hear about the earthquake?" Zahi asked.

"Heard you three talking about it. But it's not the only thing to have happened."

"What were you out looking for?" Dacia asked, furrowing her brow.

"A new town was discovered. It just appeared; seemingly out of nowhere."

"From what realm?" Dacia asked and I started.

"Second, I think. It's hard to tell with all the realms beginning to resemble each other."

"Wait so you're saying that not only are all the worlds seemingly acting as one they are actually *becoming* one?" I yelped.

Jacqueline nodded. "I'm afraid time is running out, Dacia."

"What have you found about Jacobs?" Dacia asked.

"Same thing you have, looking through these records. He was born here, lost his parents and was adopted by Deckley."

"You think that's what drove Jacobs off the edge?" Dacia murmured.

"Deckley was another traveler?" I asked, turning to Zahi. He shrugged.

"Yes, Deckley was another traveler," Jacqueline said. "But he didn't meet a very pretty end."

"What happened?" I asked, my blood running cold.

"Got on the wrong side of a financial dispute and was beheaded," Dacia summarized, covering her head in her hands and sinking into a chair.

"Jacobs took it pretty hard," Jacqueline said. "Maybe he lost faith in humanity."

"We need to find him," I said. "We need to track down Jacobs."

"No one's found him yet and it's been a long, long time since he disappeared. What makes us think we can track him down?" Zahi asked.

"I'm not sure we can," Dacia muttered.

"But we need to fix this!" I insisted.

Chapter 16

"We need to find the epicenter," Jacqueline surmised. "Where this all would have started."

"How are we going to do that? We've been looking and looking and we have nothing," Zahi pointed out unhelpfully.

We all lapsed into silence as we struggled to come up with a plan, but we were stuck. We didn't have enough information. Jacobs went missing with his three apprentices. One of the apprentices managed to get herself killed in an ancient ritual that only Jacobs and the tribe knew how to do correctly, and we'd already cleared the tribe of performing the ritual. Jacobs had lost his parents and his teacher both of which could have had major impacts on his psyche.

That didn't leave us any closer to finding him or repairing the amalgamation, only blaming the events on him. We had no other answers.

"Would it have started near where we first noticed it?" I asked.

"That's it, Alexandria. We're going about this all wrong. We need to look at the timeline. The last place Jacobs was seen was near the military base but the body we found wasn't that old. Not as old as the disappearance of Jacobs and the three apprentices."

"But the body was found near the place he disappeared. Do you think he never really left?" Zahi asked.

"I think he left, but I think he's come back at least once and that's when he disposed of the body."

"So what do we need to look for?" Jacqueline asked.

"More bodies."

{[]][]][]][]]}

When we returned to the fort we got more than we bargained for. Sandor had done as we asked and returned to his home by the river. We hadn't planned on him finding anything at the time but he'd found the other girl apprentice and sent her back to the fort with the soldier that'd accompanied him.

"You're kidding!" I exclaimed when Zahi told me the news in the mess hall.

He shook his head vigorously. "Not at all, they've got her in the med bay."

"Is she hurt?"

"Not physically but the doctors say she isn't quite all there, if you know what I mean."

"Completely insane?"

"They think its just extreme PTSD or something. Whenever they try to ask her about what happened she starts freaking out and mumbling incoherently as she starts sobbing and screaming."

"What on earth could have happened to cause such a reaction?"

"You got me. But I think this pretty much confirms sinister intent."

"Do we know it was Jacobs? Or could they have all been captured by somebody."

"Can't tell for sure, but the doctors claim that the name Jacobs does seem to be part of the mumbling."

"Has Dacia seen her yet?"

"She and Jacqueline are going to see her now."

"How old is she?" I asked, my stomach still churning at thinking of all the things she could have seen that have left scars in her mind.

Zahi shrugged. "He didn't say, though if she's like the other one, probably a little younger than us."

The other one. Suddenly I had an urge to storm to the med bay and demand to know their names, their histories. It seemed so inhuman to treat them as clues and victims. They were people. Damaged people who needed our help before it was too late. It already was too late for one of them.

"Any news on the boy?"

Zahi shook his head again, "Not a peep. The report was she was sobbing at the river's edge, though, so we might find him any day now."

I grimaced. "This needs to be solved."

"First step is to find how the pieces connect. What does sacrifice have to do with the worlds merging?"

"Maybe she'll calm down enough to tell us."

"Perhaps. Dacia can be very calming.

"Have you eaten today?"

"Grabbed an orange right when we got back."

I looked at the clock on the wall. "It's nearly seven you should eat dinner."

"I'm fine, Lex."

"When do you think Dacia will come to talk to us?"

"Dunno but if she hasn't found us by ten, I'm going to bed."

"That's three hours from now, whatch'a wanna do in the meantime?"

"I heard they were showing a movie in the gym."

"The dimensions are collapsing in on each other and you want to go to see a movie?" I asked, raising my eyebrows.

"Not much we can do about it at present, might as well enjoy ourselves while we can."

Those plans were shot, however, by Dacia walking into the mess hall.

"There you two are. Come."

"Think she wants our help?" I asked watching her retreating back.

"I think we'll find out if we follow her," Zahi teased.

I made a face and we dashed after Dacia, nearly tripping a soldier.

"Find anything?" I asked as soon as we were in earshot.

"Not as much as we'd have liked to, but the girl has been through enough. We don't want to push her more than we have to."

"We shouldn't push her at all," I said.

"With the dimensional realms merging into one we don't really have that luxury," Dacia sighed.

"Did she tell you anything at all?" Zahi asked doing a little half jog to catch back up to Dacia's brisk pace.

"It was Jacobs. He murdered the girl and the boy and was going for her next so she ran."

"Why?" I gasped.

"She said something about concealment. 'Human blood to conceal the soul' I think were her exact words."

I stopped in my tracks as my stomach decided whether or not to disgorge its contents. Zahi was lucky he hadn't eaten though he had turned a distinct greenish color.

"Alexandria? Zahi?" Dacia asked, turning around when she realized we had stopped following her.

"How could he do such a thing?" I whispered, my voice cracking.

Dacia frowned and led us to a bench.

"That's not what we're here to discover. His psychological motives are beyond us. What we need to do is to fix the balance between the realms he has disrupted."

"How?"

"We're still working on that. If you have any ideas feel free to share. But we can figure out how to do it. We know what went wrong."

"Jacobs went rogue?" Zahi clarified.

Dacia nodded. "Jacobs was one of us. Sworn to travel the realms and do what he could to help and to promote peace and wellbeing. He has murdered his apprentices and steeped himself in shrouds of death and glory. The girl, Jemma, said he plans on leading a coup into the first realm and then take his army through each of the realms in turn until they find and breach the sixth."

"That's not balance," I said. "That's not even close."

Dacia nodded. "We have to return the balance. Jemma's given us enough of a lead that we think we can find where he's hiding. One way or another we will solve this problem."

Chapter 17

Step 1. Dispose of Jacobs in a way that is the most morally correct while still being effective.

Step 2. Fix the damage he'd managed to cause. Which included, but was not limited to: somehow re-separating the dimensional realms.

Simple. Except well, it wasn't. Not even close. We still didn't know exactly where Jacobs was.

"We need more people," Jacqueline said at breakfast the next morning. "All the travelers that can come or feel they should."

"How do you contact other travelers?" I asked.

"We have our ways. We all know a few and they know a few and so on," Dacia commented. She'd been quiet for a while now and I would have given anything to know what she was thinking.

"So we get the word out, more people show up and we do what? Surround the area where we think he is and hope we find him?" I asked.

Dacia looked up and nodded thoughtfully. "That's not a bad plan of action. If we can get a little bit better of an approximation of his hideout from Jemma, then it would be easier to find."

"It would be nice to know how it's guarded as well. We don't want to lose anyone if we can help it," Zahi piped up.

And that was the first step of our plan. Jacqueline asked her commander for help and found several soldiers to act as messengers, going about the realm to various travelers Jacqueline and Dacia knew to be nearby. It was like a daisy chain message, or a game of telephone. The soldier would find a traveler, give him or her the message and return. That traveler would find another, crossing realms if needed and so on.

Meanwhile, Dacia spent time with Jemma, talking to her, helping her heal. She let her understand that the more she could tell them the easier it would be to stop

Jacobs, but past that she didn't push. If Jemma felt like sharing, she would.

It was through these discussions that we learned Jacobs had hollowed out a hill a long time ago that had been his refuge for many a year.

"How did no one know about it?" I asked.

"Our business is our business," Jacqueline shrugged. "We all have a place we can hide out if we have to."

"And no one thought he would be there when he went missing?"

"It was different."

"How so?"

"We all give off... energy signals. I guess is a way to put it. Part of your training will be to recognize them."

"Are they all alike?"

"There are subtle differences but not everyone can tell what they are. Every traveller can feel them though."

"So Jacobs 'energy signal' disappeared and that's why you thought he was missing? Do apprentices not have energy signals?"

Jacqueline squirmed. "They're not quite the same. It's something that seems to... grow. The further you get into your training the more of a signal you give off and the better you are at sensing other peoples. So when Jacobs disappeared, his signal and that of the two girls did too. But the little boy hadn't yet developed one, not enough for us to feel at least."

"What's it like, to feel them?"

"They're like, flares in the universe. I'm sure Dacia's taught you world sensing?"

I nodded.

"Well its similar. You can feel the flares just as you might be able to tell where someone is by their footsteps around the room when your eyes are shut."

"So the girls disappeared, too. One of them he killed. I assume that's what happened to her flare?"

Jacqueline nodded. "The timeline doesn't align quite like that, but death will quench a flare. That's why when one does go out we go to such lengths to find out why. Often times we're the ones to recover the body."

"And the second girl? She gives off a signal?"

"She didn't at first," Jacqueline said looking uncomfortable. "We don't know why. But it probably has something to do with how

Jacobs hid them in the first place. As she heals, though it's been coming back, stronger every day."

"Maybe we're overthinking this," I murmured.

"What do you mean?"

"Well if people who aren't travellers don't have signals/flares then maybe all Jacobs did was decide he wasn't going to be a traveler anymore. Maybe the two girls supported him at first or thought he was steering them correctly. No black magic or unknown ritualistic sacrifices. He just turned his back on the oath he made and so his flare went out."

Jacqueline furrowed her eyebrows. "You know you could just be right about that," she muttered before jumping up and grabbing her bag. "I have to go talk to Dacia. Find Zahi and meet us in the center of the base in the courtyard."

I think courtyard was a bit of a strong term for the square patch of dirt in the middle of the compound but I didn't make the names.

Jacqueline ran out one entrance to the common area and I ran out the other to find Zahi. He'd been doing the workouts with the soldiers in his spare time. I probably should have been too, but I never seemed to have enough spare time to get anything extra-curricular done.

"Zahi, meeting," I called through the door and then waited as he grabbed a sweat towel and came to follow me.

"Not going to change?" I asked eyeing his gym shorts and tank that were just a bit big. He'd probably borrowed them from one of the soldiers going off duty that weekend or grabbed them from the lost and found.

Zahi shrugged. "I figured I'd go to the meeting first. You made it sound important."

"I think it will be. We finally know where to find Jacobs."

"Then what are we waiting for?"

I was getting better at this running thing; I was only a little bit out of breath by the time we found Dacia and Jacqueline in the center courtyard.

To our surprise however they were not the only two in the square.

"'Ey guys!" Sandor called. "Meet my friends," he gestured to the five people behind him.

"Are we going to storm the hill?" Zahi asked. I had filled him in on the basics while we dashed.

"Not quite. We're waiting on a few more people that said they were comin'," Sandor said.

"So what are we going to do?"

"Plan the storm on the hill," a smallish woman said from the back. From the sound of her accent and her general appearance I guessed she was east Asian, but beyond that I had nothing. She was one of those timeless people that could be seventy-four and you'd never know. She was likely in her forties, though.

That's when the tall soldier came up to us.

"Three new reports of cities spontaneously appearing and two new reports of natural disasters, ma'am," he said bowing to Jacqueline. I guess she wasn't at the bottom of the food chain.

She dismissed the soldier almost immediately after the full report and came back over. "Whatever we're doing, we're doing it as soon as the rest of our squad gets here. We're almost out of time."

"That makes at least twenty merges in the past three days," Dacia muttered. "It's getting faster."

"How long do we have?" I asked.

"I estimate four days before it becomes critical. Max four days. Then all 'ell will break loose," Sandor said flicking cigarette ash to the ground.

"Well then," Dacia said trying to lighten the mood. "We better get to work."

{[][][][][]}

We tied the horses up under the trees so they weren't visible or in the line of fire, yet still accessible for a quick getaway. The hill wasn't exceptionally large, but it was irregular and that made the layout of the hidden cavern unpredictable. In sum total there were nearly twenty of us that spaced ourselves out around what we decided was the perimeter of the hill. With any luck we were right.

Zahi and I were on the backside of the hill. Put the apprentices where they have the least chance of getting hurt or getting in the way; that was the philosophy. Part of me wanted to ignore what they said and go to the front lines. The other part of me recognized that I did not know enough to be on the front lines and I was lucky they'd let Zahi and I come at all.

I was armed with a tranquilizer gun, though I hoped I wouldn't have to use it. Jemma swore that Jacobs would be under the hill gathering intel on various political regimes. We had gathered our own intel; none of them were close to toppling. Yet. Ergo, he must be here still.

A long slow birds whistle echoed over the landscape. Time to move in. I crept closer, keeping my eyes on the grassy mound growing in front of me.

I wasn't feeling particular lucky. In fact, had it turned out that the door to the hideout been on my side of the mountain rather than the other side where we thought it was, that wouldn't have fazed me a bit. It would have been a 'go figure' moment.

We kept creeping closer until I could only see Zahi and a young dude that had shown up at the last minute flanking me. Everyone else was blocked from my sight by the hill.

Suddenly, there was a loud cracking noise and the top of the hill blew off, showering us with bits of dirt and grass.

Chapter 17

"Go! Go!" I heard the shouts distantly, I don't know who said them, but I did as they asked and ran up the hill to the site of the explosion with my tranquilizer gun held at the ready. As we got towards the top, I could see my fellow travelers doing the same. Except those in the front of the siege. They had real guns.

The top of the hill was littered with small fires that I tried to stamp out as I came across them, but several more raged on, getting bigger as they consumed the tall, flowering grass that should have been mown months ago. If we expected to find anything at the top we were sorely disappointed. All we saw was singed dirt and we stared at the sight in silent confusion.

"Wait. Do you hear that?" Zahi asked. I frowned and listened harder. Zahi had always had super-human hearing it seemed but as I stood there I realized he was right. There was something beeping in the dirt. When the beeping began to get faster my adrenaline spiked.

"It's gonna blow!" I screamed, throwing myself away from the gap and covering the back of my neck just as the second explosion ripped the hill apart at the seams.

Dirt and rock and grass rained down covering everyone in the guts of the hill. None of the rocks were too big, but I prayed no one had gotten hit on the head. I could suddenly see Jacobs plan in my mind. He must have known we were coming; seen us or been warned. He'd lured us to the top of the hill on purpose with the expectation that the second blast would kill us.

Well, it hadn't killed me and as I struggled to my feet I was relieved to see that it hadn't killed anyone else either.

Cautiously, I approached the blast site again, inching closer and closer and listening with all my might for anything that might signal a third blast. The earth we had seen before was gone—absolutely obliterated—and the jagged scar I stood on revealed the workings of Jacobs cave underneath.

"Lex get back here!" Zahi hissed, but I ignored him, fascinated by the sight of the hollowed out hill. Slowly the other travelers approached as well.

"Well, we're no good standing out here," Dacia said.

"Adams, Langley, repel down. Avery, Michelson get to the front door. Jacqueline,

Avett cover them. Everyone else stay here," Dacia commanded.

Two of the new woman, one of the new men and Jacqueline nodded, and retreated down the hill while another woman and a man began nailing stakes into the ground with the help of Sandor.

"When you get down there, be careful. If you get into trouble we need to know about it," he grunted as he tied the ropes and tested the gear.

"Our thoughts are with you," Dacia tipped her hat and the two travelers disappeared into the shadows of the gap.

Five minutes later we heard the screaming.

"In the door!" Dacia yelled down the hill as two more travelers scrambled down the ropes for repelling.

It was agonizing to wait, listening to the action, unable to see what was going on, unable to help.

"Dacia, we have to do something!" I yelled as more screams rent the air. I couldn't tell who they belonged to but I didn't want them to be anyone's.

"We are, Alexandria," Dacia said a cold tone to her voice. "We haven't lost anyone yet."

With difficulty I relaxed and did what she was probably doing, I let my other senses take over. I couldn't see anything, fine. I could smell; I could hear. The scuffling sounded like more than nine people so Jacobs must not have been alone; how many there actually were still evaded me, though, no matter how hard I tried to concentrate.

As time ticked by, the fight found its way under the newly made skylight, and I was able to do my part. As a man broke from a struggle I could tell he wasn't part of our team; I took aim and shot him between the shoulder blades with a tranquilizer. Out for the count.

"Nice shot, Lex!" Zahi yelled.

"Which one is Jacobs?" I yelled back.

Not that Zahi knew. Sandor knew, though, and when a gangly bald man with a thick red beard stepped out of the shadows he pointed and said very clearly, "That one."

I took aim but before any of us could shoot, three travelers in the cavern attacked. There was no way to know we wouldn't hit them instead.

"We should shoot anyway!" Zahi yelled.

"If we knock out our own guys they'll be killed!" I yelled back.

Zahi frowned but he held his fire.

A few of the mercenaries ran for it, out of the circle of sunlight created by the blast and into the shadows of the mountain.

They didn't stop there, though, and as they ran out the front door I pegged one of them with a tranquilizer. The other four were being chased too closely by Jacqueline and Avett for me to get a shot in.

"Where are these people coming from?" I shouted. They seemed to be multiplying, showing up in droves and surrounding our people.

"Pull out!" Dacia yelled, shooting down a couple of stray enemy men who wandered too far from their quarry.

We still had six people down in that hole. Two began to climb the ropes, but it was too chaotic and dusty to tell who. I tried to cover them as best I could but one of them was shot in the shoulder as they climbed, despite my efforts. The person hung on, but with only one arm usable, they couldn't climb. Sandor and some other guy began hauling at the rope, trying to pull the person up.

I became preoccupied with trying to track Jacobs, who was barely visible between the flying bodies. I didn't know how these people could take so many punches and not be unconscious or dead.

Jacobs and one of our people, I think it was Adams, went down together throwing punches until I couldn't tell who was where. I kept tracking them until they disappeared. That's the first time the earth shook.

The tremor was mild and I barely lost my footing but dirt rained down on the people fighting below.

"Dacia?" I called. "Is there a fault line nearby?"

"It's getting faster!" She yelled. "And no, Alexandria. There is not."

We still had four men in the hole.

"Get out! I repeat get out!" Sandor screamed into the gap. He dropped the rope he'd hauled up back into the hole, but the two that grabbed on weren't our people. I shot one of them off and Zahi got the other.

When two more of our people reached the top, the second tremor came. This one was severe enough I couldn't keep my footing and fell on my back.

Scrambling over the warping ground to get back to the edge I was dimly aware of Zahi yelling at me to be careful. I didn't care, I needed to see what was happening. Two of our people were still in the hole. Neither was coming out. That's when the third tremor hit. If Zahi hadn't pulled me back, I would have been thrown into the hole. When I was able to get to my feet again, there was no hole, the earthquake had jammed the land together and created a fissure. Jacobs had been dispatched.

Chapter 18

The ground began to shake again and down the hill a city appeared, as if out of nowhere. One minute I was looking at green grass stretching on to the river, and then all of a sudden there was brick and mortar and streets and cars.

"Where are all these cities coming from?" I yelled across to Dacia.

"First realm," she yelled back. "It's not stopping."

It wasn't stopping. Jacobs was gone, the cause was gone, but our world was still ending. The dimensional realms were still collapsing together.

"Well what do we do?" I replied. Then I felt them. Two rifts, one on either side of the filled cavern, maybe three spread-eagled people apart. I turned to the closer one and saw a dark dismal alley in the first realm, graffitied within an inch of its life. Across from that rift I saw the familiar landscape that was the Australian outback; it must have been the third realm.

Two rifts; one to each of the realms that sandwiched the one we were in. Two rifts each with an almost magnetic pull urging me to go through. I grabbed Zahi's hand and stepped into the first realm, leaving him in the second. It was the strangest feeling I'd ever had.

I could see both worlds clearly in my mind's eye, laid out before me in all their glory. All that was there though, was a sense of chaos.

"Zahi, everyone needs to hold hands," I said my voice sounding dim and weak over the tremors and the screams. There was a loud cracking and suddenly I was standing in a darkness that couldn't possibly have been solid and the rest of the travelers with us were standing in the city that had been ripped through the dimensions.

"Zahi, hold their hands," I repeated.

Zahi looked at me with terror in his eyes, but he did as I asked, grabbing the hand of the nearest traveler and telling them to do the same. When we were all connected they understood. Dacia led her end of the line through the other rift and suddenly I could see the first three realms bumping and jostling each other for the same space.

"Not enough," I murmured as I watched cities sucked from the second realm into the third. Where buildings already stood, the newcomers blended, merging, until a skyscraper wasn't brick or iron or stone but a misshapen hodgepodge of materials stretching up into the darkening sky.

I thought of my parents and my brother and my sister and Ace and Zahi and Dacia and my extended family. There had to be a way to restore the balance between the realms.

I closed my eyes. The dark void I was in didn't hold any interest to me anymore. What I needed to see was how the dimensions fit into space and time together.

Dacia must have led the chain through another rift at that point because suddenly the fourth realm joined the fray. The once clean cities were in disarray, garbage compactors had exploded, trash and recycling cans had toppled over. There was gum on the streets, paint splashed on the buildings.

The four realms were overlapping, merging. The tremors in the ground strengthened again and I fell to my knees careful not to let go of Zahi's hand.

"Lex, Dacia says calm your mind."

"That's not the easiest thing to do right now," I replied, gritting my teeth as I tried to stay upright.

"She says calm your mind and picture the dimensional realms as they are supposed to be. Pretend you can see them as they were. Pretend that's how they are."

"Will that help?" I asked desperately.

"Dacia says we have to restore balance. We *can* restore balance. But *we* have to be balanced."

We had to be balanced. The tremors lessened and I struggled to my feet. The bruises and cuts I'd accrued stung, but I ignored the pain and the exhaustion and the desperation. I pictured the sun and the wind. I pictured rolling hills and grassy slopes for Ace. I remembered how the realms felt when they were separate and I let that memory fill my mind until it appeared to be real.

Dacia's end of the chain stepped through another rift and Zahi's hand almost slipped out of mine as the glimmering fifth realm was laid out on top of the other four.

"We're connected to all the realms. We need to balance them back out!" Zahi called. It was like a giant, telepathic game of telephone. Dacia told us what to do and is was passed down the chain of travelers until it reached me.

My eyes still shut, I pictured a scale in my mind with five hangers where weights would go. On each tray I placed one of the realms. They weren't in balance at all!

The first realm was the lightest, there was practically nothing left in it. The third realm was the heaviest, I guess because it was in the middle—that's where the convergence point was.

But how could I rebalance the scale?

I pictured the realms on the scales were different colors of clay, moldable and pliable. Ready to bend to the will of my mind. And I began to take some of the weight from the third realm scale and put in onto the first realm scale.

Slowly the balance began to even out as I redistributed the colors of clay. As I worked I noticed the clay ranged from dark to light. I put the darkest clay in the first realm and the lightest clay in the fifth realm.

But the scales just wouldn't balance. I noticed that not all of the clay felt the same. Some of the clay seemed mushier; more easily bent while other parts of the clay were hard and un-malleable.

"What on earth could be the difference?" I muttered.

I opened my eyes and was met with the dark void that was the first realm. Except it wasn't as black as before. There was grass and there were trees and there was a road.

Whatever I'd been doing—whatever everyone else had been doing—it had worked somewhat. I looked through the rift to Zahi and watched as he murmured words to himself. A great warmth welled up inside of me and I opened my free hand to the sky. I felt like an energy conduit, pulling the energy from the Universe and feeding it through the line of travelers as I fed my own energy into the dimensions.

When I closed my eyes again, I could see the five realms spread out, one on top of the other. As the energy pulsed, the dimensions moved in and out of the middle, at one point almost forming a ring before collapsing back in. I opened my eyes, but kept my mind's eye open.

Double vision; physical reality and spiritual, competing for dominance but neither would win. I kept them in balance; an eternal struggle of give and take.

The more ring-like the dimensions, the more I could see of the first realm, the more linear they got, the more I felt as if I was in an infinite chasm falling on forever. The darkness would have driven me mad had Zahi's hand not been clasped tightly in mine grounding me to what was real in the universe.

"Zahi, we need to make a ring," I muttered.

"What do you mean, Lex?" he muttered back.

"We're not all connected. We're in a line!" I said, raising my voice as the realms began trembling again. There was something different about these tremors. This time they wouldn't stop.

Zahi passed my message along the line, but still no rift opened to the fifth realm.

"Why isn't it working?" I shouted, pulling Zahi into the first realm with me as I walked forward as far as I could, searching for what could be a rift.

The ground began to buckle and sway but I refused to bow down to it. I was master here.

"Lex, what if we can't do it?" Zahi asked, stumbling.

"We can't fail, Zahi. Not when we've come so far. This is our destiny."

"Our destiny was to live normal lives and not cavort with realms and dimensions!" Zahi cried. "This is not normal. This is magic or science or something. But this can't be what we were destined to do."

"Zahi our fate was to lead ordinary lives. But we turned our backs on that long ago when we became travelers."

"Perhaps our fate is to die, Lex. Maybe the realms need to merge, maybe that's the new order of things."

"I refuse to believe that Zahi," I said shaking my head. "If our fate is to die then I do not want that fate. We *will* restore balance."

"How? There is no rift to the fifth realm. We can't complete the circle."

I stared out into the wavering, trembling darkness and was suddenly reminded forcefully of the small cell I'd stayed in for the longest time, dreaming of death or of freedom in vain, for neither came to me.

"From the darkest night comes the brightest day," I murmured moving my arm through the air as if looking for an invisible doorway. It was only after the terrors of the first realm prison that I'd been able to see and travel to the fourth realm; the realm where time fluctuated like waves upon a shore.

"Lex, your arm!" Zahi shouted. I opened my eyes and in doing so realized they had been shut. My fingers had disappeared into the dark. I moved my hand back and forth and watched as it went from visible in the gloomy light to invisible in the dark.

"What's going on, Lex?"

"I found the rift," I replied, turning and smiling at him. "I found the rift," I repeated, staring into his eyes.

"That's not the rift to the fifth realm, Lex," Zahi said shaking his head. He and I both knew that to be true. But where else could it lead?

There was only one place. And he and I both knew which one it was.

"Zahi are you ready?" I asked, a smiling playing over my lips.

He nodded vigorously. "But I sure hope you know what you're doing, Lex."

"Don't worry. I do."

"I trust you, Lex," Zahi said, he turned and pulled more travelers through the rift to the first realm. It was like someone had flicked a switch in my mind, suddenly the flares lit and I could see every one of our travelers as they stretched across the worlds. When Zahi and I stepped through the rift it would be difficult to stay connected, but it would not be impossible.

I took a deep breath and plunged into the black rift.

It obscured my vision and filled my lungs, but I was not afraid. I just kept walking until I found the light.

It was so bright after the long dark of the collapsing first realm that I had to shut my eyes, but I could still feel the rift to the fifth realm that suddenly opened not far from me. With a smile, I walked forward and stuck my hand through.

"Alexandria, where are you?" Dacia asked as she took my hand. Her voice sounded muffled through the fabric of the universe, but it was her nonetheless.

"The sixth realm, Dacia," I said my smile ever growing. "We're in the sixth realm." To keep the connection, Zahi and I both stood in the bright realm as far apart as we could and stretching until our arms ached, but we had done it. We'd connected all the realms.

"Is it beautiful?" Dacia asked, longing coloring her voice.

"It feels beautiful," I replied, still unable to open my eyes in the blinding light. "We have to balance the realms," I continued. "It's time to heal."

"The Universe is in good hands, Alexandria," Dacia said and then we talked no more as we focused on picturing the realms as they should be.

I found myself picturing the scales again, except this time there were six trays to be balanced and the clay that felt different looked different, too.

It was the clay for the sixth realm, to be separated and balanced along with all the others.

It was slow, methodical work but there was a calming, meditative feel to it that kept me patiently there, balancing the scales of the Universe.

If the tremors continued, they didn't reach me there. And my hands never fell away from my two companions, the eighteen flares in the circle never wavered.

Slowly, the six realms began to separate back into the ring. Except not all of the realms belonged in the ring. I could see that now. The sixth realm belonged at the center, connecting them all. Every time we jumped across more than one realm, we were passing through the sixth realm. All this time and nobody ever figured that out. Though really, in all the times I'd travelled we'd only skipped realms once. And it had only been Zahi and I as we escaped from the first realm to the fourth.

From darkness comes light. The easiest place to access the sixth realm was from the darkest of them all.

I pictured the balance again and realized my mistake. The balance kept all the realms in a line.

"That's not right," I said to myself with a sad smile.

I needed a circular balance and one appeared. Anything can happen in your thoughts.

One by one I transferred the realms from the straight balance to the circle balance leaving the sixth realm in the center, just like it should be.

As the last of the colored clay balls hit the balance tray, the realms separated.

We had done it. We had healed the Universe.

I opened my eyes and saw white brick stretching up in front of me. I must have been facing a wall or a building or something.

I turned to look at Zahi and saw to my surprise Ace and Fadia ambling through the rift.

"Who's my good girl," I asked Ace as she came closer to me and then proceeded to eat the grass at my feet.

"They came to us," I said.

Zahi nodded with a strange look on his face. "I don't think we're leaving quite yet, Lex," he said turning to look at me.

I nodded. "This is where we need to be right now, isn't it?"

He nodded back. "No idea why, though," he said with a shrug.

I laughed. "That's half the fun, Zahi."

He smiled and let go of the hand he was holding through the rift to the first realm with deliberation, letting it close.

But I didn't let go. Not quite then.

I turned to the rift to the fifth realm and looked Dacia straight in the eye.

"We're staying here," I said.

"I know," she said with a sad smile.

"Are you coming?" I asked though I knew she would say no.

"It is your path, Alexandria. Your path to travel with Zahi. You're on your own now."

"Dacia... my parents," I said. "Do they know I'm safe? Are they safe?"

"They're fine, Alexandria. And yes, they know you are safe. I have made sure of that."

"Will you make sure to tell them that I love them?" I asked.

Dacia smiled.

"I will tell them Alexandria, though I'm sure they already know."

I nodded, biting my lip.

"Do not worry, Alexandria. You will see them again. That is one thing that I do not have to guess."

I smiled.

"I miss them, Dacia."

"They miss you too, Alexandria. But they're proud of you. I'm proud of you as well. Both of you. We could not have restored balance to the Universe without your help."

"It was your teaching that did it, Dacia," Zahi said over my shoulder. "We owe everything to you."

"It's time for you two to make your own way in the world now," Dacia said with finality. "It's time to let go of your old teacher."

"We'll see you again, Dacia," I said.

She nodded and I let go of her hand, watching until the rift had completely shut.

Zahi and I were alone with our horses, facing the white brick wall and still holding hands. We were the only flares up here, completely on our own.

"Are you nervous?" I asked Zahi.

He thought for a moment and then shook his head. "I'm excited," he said. "We're off on a new adventure."

"Hopefully its less dangerous than the last one, right?" I joked, trying to calm the butterflies in my stomach.

"Yes, no dead bodies this time would be preferable," he replied with a forced laugh.

But still neither of us moved. Finally, I shook my head and turned to him. We had to move. If we never did, we'd never find a new purpose.

"Together?" I asked.

"Together," he said with a nod.

And so together we turned and gazed out over the marvel that was the sixth realm.

The Road That Winds Back

Chapter 18

Visit our website at
www.starlightgalaxypublishing.com
or our sister company
www.believersdreampublishing.com
for more books!

Chapter 18